MW01258231

# THE RED QUEEN

## Also by Martha Grimes

### Richard Jury series

*The Man with a Load of Mischief*
*The Old Fox Deceiv'd*
*The Anodyne Necklace*
*The Dirty Duck*
*Jerusalem Inn*
*Help the Poor Struggler*
*The Deer Leap*
*I Am the Only Running Footman*
*The Five Bells and the Bladebone*
*The Old Silent*
*The Old Contemptibles*
*The Horse You Came In On*
*Rainbow's End*
*The Case Has Altered*
*The Stargazey*
*The Lamorna Wink*
*The Blue Last*
*The Grave Maurice*
*The Winds of Change*
*The Old Wine Shades*
*Dust*
*The Black Cat*
*Vertigo 42*
*The Knowledge*
*The Old Success*

### Andi Oliver series

*Biting the Moon*
*Dakota*

### Emma Graham series

*Hotel Paradise*
*Cold Flat Junction*
*Belle Ruin*
*Fadeaway Girl*

### Other novels

*Send Bygraves*
*The End of the Pier*
*The Train Now Departing*
*Foul Matter*
*The Way of All Fish*

### Memoir

*Double Double*

MARTHA GRIMES

# THE RED QUEEN

A RICHARD JURY MYSTERY

Atlantic Monthly Press
*New York*

FIRST EDITION

*Printed in the United States of America*

First Grove Atlantic hardcover edition: July 2025

Library of Congress Cataloging-in-Publication data is available for this title.

ISBN 978-0-8021-6494-0
eISBN 978-0-8021-6495-7

Atlantic Monthly Press
an imprint of Grove Atlantic
154 West 14th Street
New York, NY 10011

Distributed by Publishers Group West

groveatlantic.com

25 26 27 28 10 9 8 7 6 5 4 3 2 1

# PART I
# Manhattan Baroque

# 1

It was all in the vermouth. She always used Carpano Antica and always a ratio of one to two, the two being whiskey from her husband's distillery. But it was the vermouth that made the difference.

"Top up your drink," said Lloyd Pruitt, barman at the Queen, "or had enough?"

The man addressed, sitting on his regular stool and looking too self-controlled and dignified to answer to the charge of "enough," must have had enough, because he lost his balance amidst calls of "Tom," "Mr. Treadnor," "What?!" and "Tom, Tom!"

No one heard it—at least not as a shot. Lloyd Pruitt, bartender and owner, later told the police he had heard something like a popping cork and couldn't remember selling a bottle of champagne that evening. To Henry Spitts, the man sitting beside Tom, the sound had registered only as a pop. To Abel Martindale, on his other side, it had sounded something like a bottle hitting the bar. Said Mervin Peake to Detective Inspector Dunstable, "We were just makin' jokes about the place bein' painted." He nodded toward the outside. "You know, it's been needin' paint for like a hundred years; it's been looking like a dump, the Queen has, and finally Lloyd got round to slappin' on a few coats."

What police had a hard time understanding was how anyone could pull out a gun in a congested place and fire it without anybody noticing. And the shooter was gone within the time it took to register with the drinkers at the bar that one of them had been shot. Only the gun hadn't been fired inside the pub, they were to discover. The gun had been fired from outside, apparently through a window. That struck the regulars as oddly amusing.

"Changed your name, did you, Lloyd?" said Mervin Peake after the commotion had died down and the police had left.

"What the hell you talkin' about, Mervin? Name's the same as ever: Lloyd Pruitt."

"Not *your* name, man; the name of the pub."

Having dropped the last of the glasses into the soapy water, Lloyd dried his hands and looked at Mervin in deep puzzlement. "What in hell—"

"Hold on," said Mervin, laughing as he went out the front door. In another minute he was back, carrying the pub sign between his hands, raising it for Lloyd to better see. "What's all this, then?"

"Well, they weren't supposed to repaint the sign."

"Then what's goin' on, Lloyd?" He raised the sign another couple of inches. Between the words THE and QUEEN someone had painted in a caret, and above it, in red paint, the word RED.

"Bloody hell!" cried Lloyd, going from behind the bar to where Mervin held the sign.

"Somebody havin' a joke at your expense, Lloyd? So now it's 'The Red Queen.' Funny it would happen the same day this guy gets shot, ain't it?"

Only the Twickenham division of the Metropolitan Police didn't find it amusing, especially not DI Dunstable, who was the only one who came. He did not need this messing up his vacation week, which was supposed to begin in three days' time. He was pretty certain it wouldn't begin unless he could search out a reason for this case not landing on his plate. In his car, before making his way to the Treadnor estate, he looked up the name on his mobile. Here he found reasons enough: Treadnor had been a rich man with some powerful friends, one of whom was the police commissioner.

There it was: the reason.

"I'm guessing he'd want Treadnor's murder handled by someone a bit further up the ladder." Dunstable was talking on speakerphone to his irascible boss, DCI Rhyms.

Rhyms took umbrage. "We're perfectly capable, man."

"Absolutely, sir. No one more than you. It's just appearances, that's all. To make things look good. This Treadnor was a big noise in the city. So you could say the case is a lot nearer to Central, couldn't you?" Ridiculous, but Rhyms could say it. He didn't want this murder on his plate any more than Dunstable wanted it on his.

By now the car had passed through the last of the lights of Twickenham and was on the road to Treadnor House. He didn't need to tell Rhyms that he didn't want the case, but he told him anyway:

"You don't want this case, sir. It's a mess. A shooting in a pub where none of the customers heard or saw anything except the body dropping to the floor."

"Very well," said Rhyms grudgingly. "I'll have a word."

"Of course, sir," said Dunstable. "I'll still be notifying his wife. I'm on my way now to his house. Another fifteen minutes and I'll be there."

Dunstable smiled and stepped on the gas and thought, Islands, here I come.

But this wasn't the Caribbean. The ground was splintered with ice, a thin sheet of it over the snow that stretched for two acres, from the low granite steps at the rear of Treadnor House and out past the barn, which now housed only three horses but had once housed ten, all thoroughbreds.

Dunstable parked, approached the house, and knocked three times. Alice Treadnor called out from the back of the house.

"Alan? Can you see who's at the door?"

"It's the police."

"What? What in God's name are the police doing here?"

"I'll let them tell you."

Treadnor House was far more a manor than a house, sitting among several acres of frozen woods and gardens and well staffed—at least if the man who came to the door was any indication. Although he was not in butler's livery, Alan Robson had all the earmarks of "butler." He led Dunstable into the house to meet Alice Treadnor. Because there was no female detective constable to go with him, this unhappy service of announcing a husband's death—worse, murder—had been left to Dunstable.

After delivering a brief account of what had happened, Dunstable went through the ritual of emphasizing that he was sorry for her loss, then gave her a few moments before getting down to business. He admired her composure. "Did you know your husband would be at the Queen? I mean, did he go there often?"

She nodded. "Yes. I assumed he was there this evening. Dinner was always a little late because he liked to stop off there."

"So you weren't expecting him home. Sorry, you just told me. Mrs. Treadnor, have you any idea if someone would want to harm your husband?"

She shook her head. "He did not have enemies. Except perhaps in his various business dealings. But don't ask me about that, as I don't really know much about his business."

"We will need to come back and have a look at your husband's things. And I should tell you that there's a likelihood of another detective from the Met coming round." He certainly hoped so.

"Why?"

"Your husband was an important man, Mrs. Treadnor, and I expect the Commissioner would want this case in the hands of a policeman from New Scotland Yard."

She said nothing, simply looking baffled. "What's wrong with Twickenham? You're still Metropolitan Police, aren't you? Is it really necessary to bring in Scotland Yard?"

He knew that it didn't make a damned bit of difference to her. She was just talking for the sake of not sinking into silence. Dunstable felt bad about his own vacation concerns. Still, he said, "Perhaps not, but my boss seems to think so. So does the Commissioner." (There, blame it on them.)

She turned away. "Then if you don't mind, I'd rather not answer any more questions."

"Again, I'm sorry, Mrs. Treadnor. I'll be going."

Dunstable went, knowing he shouldn't.

# 2

Melrose Plant sat in a leather wing chair before the fire in Boring's, waiting for the moon and the drinks to come up on the tray carried by Young Higgins, the dining room's head-waiter, if such a position existed in this private men's club.

As Melrose sat still as stone, waiting, Richard Jury said, "I've never known you to be so in need of a drink that you'd hold your breath until it came." Jury sat across from him on the other side of the fire, relaxing in a matching wing chair.

"Then you don't know me at all," said Melrose, who let out a long breath when Higgins lowered the tray.

"Thank you, Higgins," said Jury, claiming his own whiskey.

"I'll have another," said Melrose, holding out the glass, whose finger of whiskey he had emptied in one gulp.

"M'lord," said Higgins, taking it without comment.

Jury was not without comment. "Good lord, you drank that before I had a chance to raise my own to my mouth. What's going on?"

"I've had a very rough day."

Jury nodded toward the book on the table beside Melrose's chair. "Too hard, was it, holding Henry James in one hand and a glass in the other?"

James's short novel *The Sacred Fount* was stuffed between chair cushion and arm.

"Not James. Polly Praed's been on my back again to read her latest." Melrose pointed to a brown, string-wrapped parcel lying on the lower shelf of a small table to his right. "Manuscript. She's called twice. Yammer, yammer, yammer. You've no idea what Polly's like when she's trying to get you to read her stuff. And she's coming here to dinner and of course will want to talk about it."

"Why'd you invite her, then?"

"I didn't. *She* invited her."

"Why didn't you say no?"

"Me say no? I can't do it. I'm a total coward when it comes to 'no.'"

"That's absurd. You're always saying no to me."

"What? *What?* I always say yes."

"Sure. After a lot of haggling. You remember you said no to the safari, don't you? You only agreed because Trueblood was taking on the croupier's job."

"The trouble is, you go around promising people things, such as 'I know an expert in enameled mead' or 'I can get you an antiques appraiser,' thereby making it nearly impossible to refuse, as you've already stuck me with the job. Where's Higgins?"

"You're an alcoholic. When's Polly coming?"

"Too soon. Stay, please. If she sees you, she won't bother with me."

Jury was about to answer when his phone rang. He pulled it out of his pocket and saw it was Wiggins. "What is it, Wiggins?"

"A shooting in Twickenham, sir. A man named Treadnor at a pub called the Queen."

The name rang a bell, though a very small one. "Wait a minute. Twickenham has a police force. Why would the Yard be dealing with this?"

"We're all part of the Met—"

"I'm aware of that. I'm asking why *their* part of the Met can't handle it."

"This is coming down from the top, apparently. The murdered man was a friend of the Commissioner, so—"

"Only the Yard is capable of dealing with it?"

"More or less."

"I'll take less. But I expect we're stuck with more."

"Local police have been all over it—"

"So they're dealing with it. Why should we?"

"It's just orders, sir. From the Commissioner to Racer to me. Us."

Jury sighed. "Where is this?"

"Twickenham."

"I know it's in Twickenham. You said . . . Hell." Jury considered the drive, the area. "I'm at Boring's, Wiggins. Get a car and pick me up." He turned to Melrose. "Got a case. Sorry about that."

"You get a murder case. I get Polly. Lucky you." He turned to look toward the dining room. "Ye gods. Is Higgins out there distilling the stuff himself?"

"That's why the name sounded familiar. Whiskey."

"Doesn't it always? Whiskey's a popular word."

"I mean Treadnor. He makes the stuff."

# 3

It took them less than an hour to get to Twickenham and to the other side of it, where the Queen was located. They pulled up beside a police car, got out, and were approached by one of the local policemen, who told them they couldn't go in because an investigation was in progress.

Jury and Wiggins both took out their warrant cards.

"Sorry, Superintendent," said the constable.

"I'm to see Inspector Dunstable. He inside?"

"Yes, sir."

Jury stood for a few moments studying the outside of the pub, the fresh paint. Then he moved his gaze upward to a square of wood near a window. There was a slab of scaffolding beneath the window, something to hold painter and paint. There were actually several of these stationed at various points around the exterior. "Wiggins, look at this." He motioned upward.

Wiggins raised his head. "Pub sign. Someone's painted in—"

"'Red' between 'The' and 'Queen.' That's interesting."

"Wanted to rename it 'The Red Queen.' Funny."

Inside, Jury asked DCI Dunstable, "What can you tell us?"

"Victim, Thomas Treadnor, was shot in the back," said Dunstable. "And nobody saw it. Or heard it. Hard to believe."

"You're saying somebody fired a gun in here and nobody was aware of it?"

Dunstable shook his head. "We talked to everyone in the place, and no one could tell us anything."

"How many were here?"

"Twenty-six or -seven. I let people go. I didn't think you'd be getting here tonight. But I've got all their information if you want to talk to them."

"I'm sure you found out as much as I could, Inspector. What about the gun?"

"Shotgun, probably a Winchester."

"Distance?"

"Forensics hasn't given me that information yet. I'd say around thirty feet from the bar."

Jury nodded to Wiggins, who started walking, measuring off steps through the remaining patrons, who watched as if he were a fascinating new fun thing in the Queen.

"So that would be the back of the room," said Jury, seeing Wiggins stop. "Shooting through a crowd and no one noticing." He turned to the owner. "Mr. Pruitt, you heard nothing?"

"Like I told the inspector here, what sounded like a cork popping, maybe."

"Tell me, is someone larking about with you and your pub?"

"Larking? Don't know what you mean."

"Your sign, 'The Red Queen.'" Jury nodded his head toward the outside. "Can you think of anyone that might have done something like that?"

Pruitt called out over the room, "Any you morons paint the sign?"

The morons crowded up to the bar and made varying exclamations of denial. One of them said, "Lolly? Maybe Billy or Wen?"

"Don't be daft. They'd never be so dumb. They wouldn't get paid for the job, and maybe not get another one ever round here, doin' something like that."

"I take it you're talking about the painters?"

Pruitt nodded. "Brothers. They do a lot of painting in Twickenham. Wendell and Billy."

Jury turned to Dunstable. "You talk to them?"

Dunstable shook his head. "I didn't see the sign."

"I mean more generally, talk to them in relation to the pub, the shooting."

"No."

Jury turned to the man sitting on the bar stool to his right, who had said his name was Mervin Peake. "Mr. Peake, you were sitting here next to Mr. Treadnor, right?" When the man nodded, Jury went on. "Did you talk to him?"

"Yeah, a little bit, but nothing important."

Jury smiled. "Suppose you tell me the unimportant."

"Oh, about his car and how the transmission seemed to be giving him trouble and how he wasn't looking forward to getting that bill. Then about cats, the old pub cat that comes and wraps around your legs sometimes and how he didn't like cats. Dogs neither. A big nuisance."

Jury went back to Dunstable and drew him aside. "You came back from the Treadnor house. How did that go?"

Dunstable took out his notebook. "Alice is the wife. She took it, I'd say, pretty calmly. Still, I didn't want to question her a lot in the circumstances. Just asked if she could think of anyone who'd want to do him harm."

"And she knew of no one."

"That's right. I didn't find out much."

"That's okay. I'll have to find it out for myself. Thanks, Inspector."

Dunstable put away the notebook that hadn't afforded him much. "Funny thing, though."

"What's that?"

"There wasn't a lot of grief in that house." He looked around. "Or anywhere else I can see."

* * *

Somebody was grieving.

This was Sally Todd, bar girl at the Queen. She could barely keep the tears out of the pint she was drawing for a customer. "Can't believe it, I can't." She stopped pulling the tap handle to snuffle into a tissue, which she then tossed away, then pulled at the Guinness tap again. After drawing the pint of beer, she reached into the cooler to pull out Sergeant Wiggins's orange squash.

Jury didn't know there still was such a thing. "Haven't seen one of those in years, Wiggins."

"You're drinking in the wrong places, boss." This comment was accompanied by a wink at Sally Todd.

Jury rolled his eyes.

"Horse's arse," said a rake-thin man who dropped five quid on the bar and asked for a beer.

Sally's color went up more than a notch. "Never you mind, Mick, now Tom's dead. And you never did an honest day's work round here, neither."

"Mebbe, but I never stole from a blind man's tin cup, did I, Sal?" He laughed as she snapped the bar rag over her shoulder at him.

Observing the interaction, Jury remarked to Wiggins: "Mr. Treadnor seems to call up slightly different feelings in different people, doesn't he?"

Lolly was back with the names of the painters written on a piece of paper, which he handed to Jury. "Can't see you'll get any joy outta them, sir. When they were done, I looked the job over, and the sign hadn't been touched." He shook his head. "Beats me, man."

There were half a dozen drinkers now circled around the one called Nick, mumbling and speculating. "Some kind of message, you think?" one asked.

"I've no idea," said Wiggins.

"Accusing somebody, then?"

"Maybe, but of what?"

"Given that guy, could be anything from a generous knight to an arrogant arse."

Jury was going to stop this last contributor to the picture of Treadnor but decided to wait.

One of the crew who had gathered broke away from the others and said, "I'll tell you something, Inspector" (any policeman being "Inspector" to those who weren't too familiar with rank), "that man deserves a knighthood, make no mistake. He was—"

"An' I'm bloody Prince Charles, Freddie, that's what."

"Come off it, Jim; Treadnor put my kid straight through the University of London business school, no questions asked, just when my boy lost that scholarship."

"Yeah. Well, that was a one-time gift," said Jim.

There was more disagreement, and it looked for a few moments as if sides would be chosen up and chairs churned to dust until Lloyd stepped in to shut them up.

# 4

Detective Superintendent Richard Jury was introduced with his rank intact when he met Alan at the door of Treadnor House. Jury was merely amused by the formality, not being used to the world of butlers, except for Melrose Plant's. Ruthven must surely have been the prototype for all of them.

The room Jury was led into was lined with bookcases. He guessed it to be a library or a study. It was densely populated with shadows. The only source of light was a fireplace and one floor lamp. The rear of the room was so lost in shadows, he could barely make out the form of the woman who spoke his name. "Mr. Jury?" she said.

"Mrs. Treadnor."

" 'Alice' will do." She moved to a table that was lined with bottles and decanters, one of which she removed the glass top from, and said, turning her back to him, "Care for one? It's just whiskey."

" 'Just whiskey' is exactly what I'd like—just not too much of it, please."

She poured a couple of fingers into each of two cut-glass tumblers. "Won't you sit down?" She handed him one of the glasses. There were two facing sofas. He took one of them; she sat, still in shadow, on the other.

"I'm terribly sorry about your husband." She said nothing, but even her silence was composed. He thought she was a person of great composure, and he told her so.

She sipped her whiskey and said, "Composure? Or simply lack of feeling?"

That surprised Jury, until he remembered DS Dunstable's comment: There wasn't a lot of grief in this house. Still, her calm admission of this apparent absence of grief was surprising.

"There wasn't a great deal of love here, at least not on Tom's side. We were going to get a divorce. I really loved him. He didn't love me. He admired me so much, I guess it looked to everyone who knew us like love." She raised her glass. "Another?"

He tapped the whiskey still visible in his glass and shook his head. She went to the drinks table and poured more whiskey from the same decanter. Holding up her glass, she said, "This was one of our problems."

Jury said nothing.

"My drinking, not his." She took the glass back to the sofa and sat down again.

Jury said, "What was another problem? Other men?"

She looked at him with astonishment. "Other men? Were there any other men with Tom around? Tom was the most charming man I've ever known. Tom was all charm. No man could compete with him. You didn't know him. Another problem was that he found me inscrutable." She said this as she sat by the arm of the sofa. She fairly melted into a shadow.

"Inscrutable?" said Jury.

"That's how Tom described me."

"So he felt you were unknowable."

"You can't understand that?" she said.

"Yes, but then, I feel most people are." That made her laugh.

"Even a detective can feel that way?"

"Oh yes," said Jury. "But I can't see its calling for a divorce. Was this divorce imminent?"

"Yes, Tom had his lawyer ready."

"And what about you? Was yours ready?"

"You mean, to contest the divorce? No. It would have been useless. And really, what would have been the point."

Jury said, "The point was that you loved him." Into the silence that followed, Jury said, "Were you at the Queen the night of the shooting?"

She shook her head. "No."

"Do you go there often?"

"Hardly ever. Tom is a regular. I am not."

"Your husband has a lot of business dealings; can you think of anyone who would've wanted him out of the way?"

She gave an abrupt laugh. "Out of the way? Maybe. But not dead. He recently had a serious disagreement with Brad Ross, who has been his business partner for years."

"About what?"

"A project called Land Savers," said Alice.

Jury asked, "What's that?"

"It would be more to your benefit to ask Mr. Ross."

"This Mr. Ross, where will I find him?"

"He lives not far from here, about a quarter of a mile down the road. A big house. Georgian architecture, I think."

Jury took a last sip of his whiskey and said, "Thanks very much, Alice." He rose. She looked at him, and for some reason a line from a Philip Larkin poem came into his mind: *Like something almost being said.*

She said, "You're smiling. Why?"

"It's just a line of poetry I've always liked," he said, and he told her what it was. Then he turned and walked toward the door held open by Alan. He stopped when he heard her voice.

"Perhaps it was."

"It was?" He took a step toward her. He felt compelled to stay and compelled to leave.

Leaving won. He went through the door that Alan held open. He left the house, got into his car, and went to pick up Wiggins. Together they drove to Ross's.

# 5

The person who came to the door of the Georgian house was Eleanor Ross herself. No butlers here—though Jury supposed that was not for lack of funds, but for not wanting to put out some other member of her staff unnecessarily.

"Mrs. Ross." Both Jury and Wiggins pulled out their IDs for her inspection. "Could we have a word with you and your husband?"

She gestured for them to come in. "Of course. Although I expect a word is far less than you really want."

"What more, then?" asked Jury. She looked puzzled. "What more do you think we want?"

Now she laughed slightly. "My husband has been on the phone most of the morning. I will just get him. He is in his study."

They went through a doorway into a lavish kitchen, where a very thin woman was working at the stove.

"Hilda, I want you to meet somebody." Hilda turned and looked expectant. "This is Superintendent Richard Jury of Scotland Yard. He has come to talk to Brad, and I wanted him to meet you."

"Certainly, sir." Hilda extended her hand and Jury shook it.

Eleanor said, "Hilda has been Ross's cook for over forty years. She has been in the family longer than that. She makes the most wonderful soufflés."

"Thank you, ma'am," said Hilda. "But there is something you must be careful about when it comes to a soufflé."

"What's that?" said Jury.

"You have to be careful that you eat it right away."

At that moment, Brad Ross was out of his study and coming toward them with his hand outstretched. He said, "You must be the detectives Eleanor told me about."

Jury said, "I am deeply sorry about your partner—"

Brad waved the sorrow away as he ushered them into the study and had them sit down. Eleanor followed them.

"To tell the truth, Superintendent, my wife is more of a fan of Tom than I am."

"Brad!" exclaimed his wife. "That's hardly fair."

"What?" he said. "That you are, or that I'm not?"

"Really, Brad. Tom's been your partner for nearly twenty years! How can you say that? You shared that office with Tom in the city all this time."

"Where in the city, Mr. Ross?" asked Jury.

"You know, the famous building. Looks like pickle. Right on 30 Saint Mary Axe. We have a third partner, McPhee."

Jury decided not to ask Eleanor Ross to leave, but said instead, "Perhaps we can begin with why you're not."

"I beg your pardon?" said Brad.

"A fan."

Brad's laugh sounded more embarrassed than amused. "Well, the final decision for anything was down to him. So if I disagreed—"

"You lost," said Wiggins, opening his notebook and clicking his ballpoint pen.

"That's right."

"But the company now belongs to you, Mr. Ross," said Wiggins.

Brad half laughed. "Well, I guess that makes me a suspect, doesn't it?"

"Oh, I expect you already were, sir." Wiggins smiled, ignoring Jury's icy look.

"You disagreed. An example of this disagreement?" said Jury.

"The most recent acquisition, which we called Land Savers. Both of us are—were—strong on conservation. The idea was to buy up good land, forested land, to keep it out of the hands of developers. Then a few months later, Tom decided we should build a few houses. That strikes one as contradictory, doesn't it?

I pointed this out. We argued for a long time, but, as I said, Tom had the last word. He always did."

Eleanor said, "Brad, you signed the contract. You didn't have to."

"You're right. There was just something about the guy that simply made you trust him. Even if you had been fooled before." Brad shrugged. "The man was manipulative. But still, there was something so disarming about him."

"And you had been fooled before, Mr. Ross?"

"Oh, yes." He ran his thumb across his brow as if teasing out a reason for his own behavior. Then he said, meditatively, "Shot in the back in a bloody pub. My God."

"Perhaps he fooled the wrong person," said Jury.

"Yes. Perhaps."

"Or maybe he didn't."

"Didn't what?"

"Fool him."

Brad went to the drinks table and offered whiskey to Jury and Wiggins, who both hastily shook their heads.

"You've talked to Alice Treadnor?"

"Yes, of course."

"I imagine you found her impenetrable."

"What a strange thing to say about Alice," Eleanor said.

Surprised, Jury said, "On the contrary, I found her to be rather transparent."

Brad laughed. "Transparent? Alice?" He turned with a whiskey in his hand and said, "Alice is shadows and fog. You cannot see through her."

This truly puzzled Jury. "But you can see through fog if you turn on the lights." Then, abruptly, Jury said, "Well, thank you for your time, Mr. and Mrs. Ross. We will be going."

As they parted, Jury wondered if it might be Alice who upset Brad more than Tom did.

Eleanor Ross said, as she showed them out, "You know, Brad is really far more upset over Tom than he lets on."

Jury smiled. He doubted this. "Thank you, Mrs. Ross. You will see us again, I imagine."

Her false little smile became falser. "Oh, yes. Well, anything we can do to help."

# 6

Jury picked up Wiggins the next morning in the same place he had left him, standing on the curb outside of his flat.

Jury said, "The office is in the Gherkin, 30 Saint Mary Axe."

"The Gherkin?"

"That's not the official name, Wiggins. It's an astounding piece of architecture, and we call it a pickle. You ever been in it?"

Wiggins said brightly, "Nope. I hope they have pickle parking."

"I'm sure they will," said Jury.

They found the building in a very busy part of the city. They parked and went into this architectural wonder of green glass.

For a rich man, Tom Treadnor kept an office decidedly modest, though his secretary was anything but. She was pretty much bursting the bounds of gorgeousness, with flaming-red hair artfully restrained by combs and a thin ribbon, and a body that could not be restrained by the simplicity of the dark suit she was wearing. And to top it all or bottom it all off, looking at her in the shadows of her semicircular desk, Jury saw a small deskplate indicating that her name was Amber.

Amber must have been the office's star attraction. If Tom T. was a lady's man, here was the lady.

Jury said, "I'm sorry about Mr. Treadnor. I understand he had a partner."

"Two," said Amber. "Abner Smith and John McPhee. Abner's out right now, but John is here. I'll get him." Amber pushed the button on the intercom. "Mr. McPhee. There's a policeman here—a Detective Superintendent Jury, New Scotland Yard."

McPhee came down a short hall behind them. They shook hands and he waved them toward his office. Jury turned to Wiggins and suggested he stay and question Amber.

McPhee's office was as understated as the reception area, except it was full of papers, books, and magazines, yet very neat and compact.

McPhee began with a fairly standard expression of disbelief at the impossible shooting of his partner. "No one could have had any reason . . ."

"But he must have had adversaries."

"Adversarial relationships, yes, but not murderous ones."

"Did you agree with his land-buying pursuits?"

"Most of the time, yes."

"What about the rest of the time?"

"Well, I found it rather self-promoting."

"Odd word," said Jury.

McPhee corrected this and said, "Self-righteous generosity. And he lately decided we should think about building on this land—houses. Modest, of course."

"In other words, development. The very thing he was rallying against."

McPhee nodded. "No accounting for this change of mind, really."

"I seriously doubt this had anything to do with the shooting."

"No, that sounds more personal."

"Talk about the personal, then," said Jury.

McPhee puffed his cheeks out in apparent frustration. "I didn't know Tom that well. I wasn't close to him. He wasn't a man who talked much about his feelings."

Jury said, "But the implication surely is that Alice and Tom did not always get along."

"Do any two people always get along?" McPhee moved around in his chair in discomfort. "Well, you know I hate to speculate."

"I know you hate to, but I'd appreciate it if you did."

"I believe divorce had its hand in the air."

"Any other hands up? His? Hers?" Jury moved his own hand up in the air.

"You mean, which hand if either was going to shake on the divorce?"

"That's what I mean, Mr. McPhee."

"Do you always talk in such runic messages, Mr. Jury?"

"No, but you're the one who started it. You put your hand up in the air. I'm sorry. I just want to know which one of them wanted the divorce. Maybe both. I don't know."

"Well, I can tell you it wasn't both. The one who wanted it was Tom."

"Do you know why?"

"Oh, I guess it's all pretty muddy. There must have been a hundred reasons."

"Can you tell me any of them? If not a hundred, ninety-nine."

"I think he found Alice was too . . ."

"Too what?"

"Too observing or observant. She was always watching."

"That's interesting. I don't think I've ever heard that before."

"She was good at figuring or working things out about people. You know, analyzing. You're a policeman. You know what I mean."

"Maybe not about Tom Treadnor, though."

Jury smiled, realizing he wasn't going to get more out of McPhee. "I guess I'll gather up my sergeant and leave, but I'll certainly be back to see if you've remembered any other possibilities."

# 7

Jury and Wiggins left the Gherkin building for a six-minute walk to Tower 42. Jury stopped and looked toward the top. "Come on, Wiggins, let's go in."

"In where, sir?"

"Vertigo 42."

"That's a bar."

Jury sighed. "Not just any bar, Wiggins. A champagne bar with panoramic views of London. It's one of the tallest buildings in the city. It's sensational."

Wiggins, not moving, was pointing instructively at his smartphone's clock. "It's barely gone eleven, sir."

"Right. Just the time for a glass of champers. Come on." Jury pulled him through the door into the glassy and glittery environs of Tower 42. Not glittery in *fact*, thought Jury, but in feeling. They made their way to the tiny elevator—one stop. "I love it. Vertigo, the bar."

"We are on duty," said Wiggins sententiously.

"Right. And we're doing it." The ascent of the elevator was so fast it seemed not to be moving through air. At the top, the door opened noiselessly, and they stepped into the soft arena of Vertigo 42, famous for champagne and for its spectacular views of London. It's what people came here for: to drink and see London among the stars. The lozenge-shaped room was entirely surrounded by windows, with a wide glass ledge that ran round it and served as a series of tables.

He'd been here several times with Phyllis Nancy—indeed, once when her dress had furnished the clue to solving the case he'd been working on and once when he'd met Tom Williamson, whose case it had been. Vertigo 42 served up many good memories, not the least of which was champagne, although for a headier vintage than Jury could afford. He remembered Tom Williamson could easily afford the headiest, and had.

When Wiggins noted this sky-high cost, his eyebrows nearly went up to the ceiling. "Good God, sir! Do you see these prices?"

"It's on New Scotland Yard, Sergeant. Just a glass." The prices went up as dizzyingly as the elevator.

"Just a glass is what I'm looking at. I could get a glass of juice."

"Perhaps. And it would cost just as much, I bet." Jury gestured to the waiter, from whom he ordered two glasses of what appeared to be the cheapest of the lot. The lot ran to fifteen pounds per. "Pull your eyeballs back in, Wiggins. I'm buying."

Wiggins asked the waiter if he could have half orange juice in his champagne.

The waiter did not seem to know whether to laugh or cry, so he did neither. Stoically, he poured, saying, "I'll return with your orange juice, sir."

Everyone in the room appeared to be reading the *Financial Times*. There was one *Telegraph* reader in the seat next to him, and before the man turned the page, Jury saw a photo of Tom Treadnor, but he couldn't make out the caption beneath it. Jury asked the waiter if he could bring him a copy.

"Certainly, sir." The waiter went immediately to the front desk to fetch it.

"What's that?" said Wiggins, crinkling his nose as he tasted the champagne.

"Sorry it's not a Bruit, Wiggins." Jury folded back the sheet to see the photo. "Story about Tom Treadnor." Except it wasn't a story about Treadnor. It was a picture. Jury was astonished; the name beneath the picture was Jason Lederer. Jury put his thumb across the name and turned the page so that Wiggins could see it. "Who is this, Wiggins?"

Wiggins glanced at it. "Tom Treadnor. Why? Didn't they get the story right?"

"Nothing to do with the story. It's the man. Look." Jury removed his thumb.

"But that's impos— It's clearly Treadnor. Paper must've mixed up the photo and the caption."

"Nope. Story's about this Lederer guy moving from his job here and going to his firm's other office in the States. Seems to be the CFO of a small company stationed in a building just up Broadchurch Street. Amazing resemblance to Treadnor, isn't it? Could be twins."

"Well, if Tom had a twin brother, Alice would have said," said Wiggins.

"Someone would have." Jury folded the paper, shoved it in his coat pocket. "Come on."

"On where?"

"To where this Jason guy was working. We want to find out about him."

"Haven't finished my drink, sir." Wiggins picked up the glass and took a swig.

"Too early for you. Come on." Jury paid his bill and they returned to the elevator and its speedy descent.

# 8

"Bygones," said Jury. "Do you think that's a good name? Strikes me as rather dismissive, or at least past tense."

"It's just a play on words. On *a* word, I mean."

"I know that, Wiggins, but it still seems negative. Or maybe a good name for an antiques shop or consignment place. But not a travel agency. It's a big one, according to the *Financial Times* article. There's several around here in London."

"Are we going to stand out here discussing the name, or go inside and discuss this Jason guy?"

"Thanks, Wiggins, for pointing out my time-wasting proclivities."

"Well, we could stand out here and discuss those too."

"Don't push your luck," said Jury, pushing at the revolving door in Broadchurch Street.

Wiggins ha-ha'd and revolved with him.

Inside, the guard, or whatever he was, and he was one of many—all of these buildings made it appear as if a robbery were in progress or about to be—responded immediately to Jury's warrant card and told him where they could find the Bygones headquarters. They took the escalator to the third floor. Bygones was on the other side of a door with a partly frosted window.

Behind a beautifully molded desk stood a similarly well-molded blonde. The warrant card had the same effect on glamor as it had on security and, following a very brief interoffice phone call, they were ushered into the office of the acting CFO.

"Ah, Jason!" said Mr. Davies enthusiastically, almost as if Jury were Jason himself. "Yes, Jason left for Chicago over a week ago. Why? What's he done?"

This was often the jokey response to Jury's identifying himself as New Scotland Yard CID. Jury said, "Nothing I'm aware of. Except that a man murdered in a Twickenham pub looked exactly like him."

"My God! He was on his way to Chicago, and he didn't get any farther than Twickenham?"

No end to the jokes. "The victim didn't. I don't know about Mr. Lederer. Now, could we get serious for a moment? I saw Mr. Lederer's photo in the *Financial Times* and was astonished for a moment because I thought it was the man who'd been shot. His name was Tom Treadnor."

"Christ! That explains it," said Davies as he slapped his hand on his desk so hard the ink stand jumped.

"It does?"

"Jason and this Treadnor have been confused before. I mean, one for the other. I think Thomas Treadnor worked in the Gherkin—I mean, you know . . ."

"Number 30 Saint Mary Axe. Yes, I know it. But can you tell me more about Jason Lederer? His personal life? Family?"

"Well . . . no wife, no kids. No, I always assumed Jason enjoyed his bachelor status." Mr. Davies smiled ruefully, as if he wouldn't mind sharing in such a status. "Of course, he had women . . ."

"Any woman in particular?"

"Stuff like this I wouldn't know. See, we weren't on intimate terms. I mean, such that he'd talk to me about his love life."

"How long was he here in this job?"

"Two years, I think."

"Why did he go to Chicago?"

"Headquarters wanted him to. They're setting up a Chicago office. I think they want to expand in the U.S. with a number of offices."

"Could you tell me where this office is? I mean, the Chicago address?"

"Sure." Davies flipped on the intercom and asked the glamorous woman at the desk to find the address and tell him. Then he switched off the intercom and said, "I'm not sure I understand all of this, Superintendent . . ."

"Jury. I'm not sure I do either."

The woman outside turned on her intercom and gave the address, which Wiggins heard and wrote down.

Jury rose. "Thank you for your time, Mr. Davies." Jury held out a card. "My card. In case you think of anything at all that might be helpful."

Davies said, "The man who was shot . . ." Not happy that Jury had come, Davies now gave the impression that he was not eager to see him leave. "Do you think they knew each other?"

"No. Are you sure Lederer is in Chicago? I mean, have you talked to him since he left?"

"No, but there'd have been no reason to, really."

"You've got his job. I'd think there'd be every reason. Your business must run very smoothly otherwise."

"The transition has been, I'd say, extremely smooth. Remember, I was Jason's assistant for years."

"I didn't mean to suggest you weren't competent to handle it, but the loss of a CFO, I'd think, would impact any business."

"Not really. It's just a job."

"No, it isn't. You're a modest man, Mr. Davies." Jury rose. "And we've taken up quite enough of your time. Especially unannounced."

"Oh, I'd say an unannounced visit from Scotland Yard would make anyone's day."

"No, you wouldn't."

"Do you always contradict people?"

"Yes," said Wiggins. "Thank you, sir." He held out his hand and shook with Davies, who laughed.

Back on Broadchurch Street, Jury said, "I'm astounded by the information I'm not getting."

"But why would you expect to get it if there's nothing to get, at least in the case of this Lederer?"

"Except . . ."

"Except what? He just looks like Treadnor, that's all. They say that each one of us has a look-alike somewhere in the world. I think that's rather nice, don't you?"

"Not in your case."

"Oh, thanks."

Jury laughed. It was just payback for the comment about contradiction.

# 9

A tallish, youngish man bending over a bed of primulas looked up as the police car stopped in front of the entrance.

Looked up, but without apparent interest, and looked down again. The lack of interest was a ruse, since no one would lack interest in the police at their door.

Alan opened the door.

"Oh," he said, "you again."

Jury smiled. "Us again."

"I'm afraid Mrs. Treadnor is a little too busy to see you now." His tone was smug.

Jury's tone was even more smug. "No, she isn't. That is, if it were her we wanted. But it isn't. May we come in?"

Very puzzled, Alan stood back, making an unenthusiastic gesture to enter. "Then who?"

"You, Mr. Robson. I want to talk to you." Why did the man look surprised? It should be obvious police would question everyone connected with the house.

"Please don't speculate, Mr. Robson. We'll be all day at it if you do." Jury turned to Wiggins. "Begin with the cook, Wiggins."

Alan raised his eyebrows. "Cook?"

"You're not going to tell me you don't have one? Cook or chef? I assume she or he is in the kitchen. So, where's that?"

Eyebrows back in place, Alan nodded toward the back of the room. "Come this way, Sergeant."

Wiggins went. Jury waited until Alan was back. "Where can we talk?"

"The office." He turned again.

The butler has an office. Things had certainly changed.

It was quite a nice one too. Leather furniture, large desk. Jury wondered if this was, in fact, Tom's office.

Both of them seated, Alan said, "How can I help you, Superintendent?"

There was something mildly patronizing in that. "I'd like to know if you have any idea as to why your boss was murdered."

"He was a friend more than a boss. The answer is no. It's unbelievable. How could anyone in that place have shot a gun without anyone noticing immediately, so that the shooter could get away?" When there was no answer, Alan went on. "You're asking if anyone had a reason to shoot Tom Treadnor?"

"Yes, but in a more general way: What was he like?" Jury waited while Alan helped himself to a cigarette from a silver box. He did not pass the box to Jury.

"When I met Tom, I'd been out of work for a year, couldn't find any kind of job. After a few hours and a few drinks in a pub, he offered me a job." Alan pointed at the floor. "This job. Butler. I told him I had absolutely no experience with that kind of thing, and he said, 'Hell, Alan, anyone could do that sort of thing. What it takes is an ability to project, I don't know, maybe humility.'"

"Subservience" would say it better, but Jury didn't, at least not in that way. "You don't strike me as a man who would deal well with that, Mr. Robson."

Alan laughed abruptly. "I was hardly in a position to deal at all, was I?"

"Maybe not then, but your job turned into a years-long one. Was he all right to work for?"

Surprised that anyone could question Treadnor's "all rightness," Alan said, "My lord, of course."

"You didn't think he was being exploitative?"

"What? Tom? My God, no. What would make you say— Let me just say something: Tom was the best person I've ever known. Anyone would tell you that."

"But that's the point, Mr. Robson, 'Anyone' hasn't. Indeed, there seems to be a number of *anyones* who disliked him."

"Exploitative? That would be coming from Brad Ross, I'll bet. Brad was the business partner, the one who knew far less than Tom about business. So that might be put down to simple jealousy. Look, I'm more than a butler. I practically run the place. I hire and fire; I have the final say over who works here, how they do, et cetera."

Much like Treadnor himself.

"You admired him?"

"I did."

"Why?"

He didn't answer for a few moments.

Finally, Jury spoke through the silence. "I'd better collect my sergeant, Mr. Robson. Could you direct me to the kitchen?"

# 10

In the kitchen, Wiggins was having some tea, seated at the table with a middle-aged woman who was aproned and looking very cookish. "Elsie Bloom," said Wiggins by way of introduction.

Elsie Bloom could have been the platonic ideal of "cook," with her white apron strings wrapped around her middle at least twice and flour halfway up to her elbows.

From the bowl beside her she took small, roundish things Wiggins took to be dumplings—bites?—that she rolled in the flour.

They had been through the preliminaries regarding Tom Treadnor ("Mr. Tom" to Elsie). "Oh, he was all right," she had said, suggesting somebody else wasn't. "I'm awful sorry he's gone."

But Treadnor's goneness wasn't interfering with the speed of the flour-coating. Wiggins wondered what it had been about Tom Treadnor that he failed to cause any despair in a cook who had been with him for nineteen years. And had clearly enjoyed it.

Her dipping stopped suddenly. "But shot like that? No, I can't believe it." The dipping continued.

"Somebody certainly didn't like him, Elsie. The question is, who. He appeared to be a popular man, for the most part."

"It's the other part makes you wonder, though." She stopped again, staring off into space, frowning.

"What is it?"

She shrugged. "Oh, nothing."

"What are you making there?"

"Bites."

Well, he'd got one thing right. Then he said, "Who takes care of the horses, Elsie?"

"Rufus Stewart. He's the stable man."

"Is he here now?"

"Should be. Stable's just out there." She nodded toward the rear of the house. Then she picked up the jar of Nutella. "Tommy, Mr. Treadnor's great-nephew, loves this. Funny, Mr. Treadnor did too, but he seems to have gone off it. Elsie dropped her head. "I keep forgetting, he's—" She went on looking down at the jar as if the Nutella might have had something to do with Treadnor's death. She took the jar to a cabinet and stuffed it in.

# 11

The man that Jury found standing in front of the cooker was tall and elegant, but not in chef's costume. The cuffs of his light blue shirt were rolled back, and the pants were a crumpled khaki. In a large black frying pan, he was stirring around onions and cucumber sliced so thin it looked transparent.

The man turned to Jury and looked at the ID he held out.

"Mr. Santos?"

"New Scotland Yard?" said Santos. "The Met is really turning out the big guns. Did Twickenham police get trampled in the process?"

"Not at all," said Jury. "Inspector Dunstable is a perfectly capable detective."

Jury looked at the thin slices of cucumber Santos had produced.

The chef turned from the Aga, went to the refrigerator, took out a small, brown-paper-wrapped package, and tossed it on the butcher-block table in front of the Aga.

Jury watched him open it and said, "Fish? Is that what the cucumbers and onions are for?"

"Your talents are being wasted, Superintendent Richard Jury. Anyone that intuitive should be in the kitchens of the Goring Hotel."

Jury answered, "Leave out the word 'intuitive' and my boss would probably agree with you." While Jury watched the delicate maneuvering of the sole into the pan with the other ingredients, he said, "The shooting was extremely difficult and very well-thought-out."

Santos turned the fish and said, "Very delicate, almost as delicate as the sole."

"Do you consider yourself capable of such an operation?"

Santos looked at him and laughed. "Probably, but I was here hovering over a mushroom quiche."

"Ah," said Jury. "And do you happen to know where Mrs. Treadnor might have been hovering that night?"

"Well, I do know she was in the house that night. She was here on and off."

"Any time frame connected to that 'on and off'?"

"Well, I know she was here when I was shucking the oysters, and that was around sixish."

"And around sixish was the last time you saw her that night?"

"She was back when I was assembling the oyster salad."

"And what time was that?"

"That would be around seven p.m., and I'm afraid that's all I can tell you. Until later that night, when I saw her in the kitchen around midnight with a glass of brandy."

"What about the rest of the staff?"

Santos said, "Were they with us having a glass of brandy?"

"No, did any of them mention if they'd seen her?"

"That I'd have to think about."

"Aren't the onions overcooked by now?"

Santos smiled at him as one might at a child.

"Oh, sorry. I just noticed some burnt bits."

Santos raised his eyebrows; Jury was afraid that God might be doing the same thing.

"Burnt bits are part of the dish."

"Really? I've never heard of a dish that called for burning—"

"Shall I get you an apron, Superintendent?"

Santos reached for an apple in a wire basket and started slicing it with the same precision he had used with the cucumber, and with the same speed.

"I get the impression Mrs. Treadnor likes anything you cook."

"She does, yes."

"Are you adding apples to the pan?"

"Are you getting this information for Mrs. Treadnor? She's always trying to guess what's for dinner."

"No, I'm just curious. It looks delicious."

"I'm curious too. Have you got a lead on who shot Tom Treadnor?"

Jury ignored the sarcasm. "No, I intend to go to the stable and talk to your stable master."

# 12

Jury was surprised that a stable housing four horses could be so neat. He observed a youngish man who was hunkered down beside one of the four, wiping him down with a towel.

After identifying himself, Jury asked the man if he was Rufus Stewert.

"Just Stewert, if you don't mind. I've never liked my first name, but since I don't have a middle one, I expect I'm stuck with it."

"Do they—did they ride all of these horses?"

"Yeah, except for the gray over there." He nodded in the direction of the last stall. "That belongs to the Rosses. Their friends. Ross doesn't have a barn. The Treadnors keep it as a favor."

Stewert's headshake suggested this was pretty unthinkable, not to have a barn if you had a horse.

"I'm surprised Mr. Treadnor had the time for riding, given his multiple jobs."

"Yeah, well, he wasn't very good at it. Tom sat in the saddle like a sack of potatoes."

Another headshake. Another horse transgression.

"I never understood it: to own three horses and you don't master the simple art of mounting."

Jury smiled. "If it's an art, it's not simple."

"Maybe. Well, he got a lot better at it just before he died. As if he suddenly got it." Stewert shifted his eyes for several seconds. "Sorry. The whole thing's terrible. Terrible."

"How about her? Is she a good rider?"

"Very good." He was standing now, the towel slung over his shoulder.

"You like her? And aside from his poor riding, did you like him? I mean beyond 'He was all right'?"

Stewert was inspecting the hooves of the horse and didn't answer for a few moments. Jury concluded that the job was allowing him time to think. "No."

That was the tense and emphatic answer.

"Why?"

Stewert stood up. "I can't . . . He was too unpredictable. A real changeable temper. Like, when I knew he was going to ride, I'd get a horse ready, one that he'd said he really liked—the

Andalusian over there." He nodded toward the gray horse in the last stall. Then he'd say he didn't like it and didn't I know by now to saddle up the quarter horse—that's the second one."

Jury looked at the horse in the second stall. It was a beautiful chestnut color.

"'But you said you liked the Andalusian,' I'd say. 'I can change my mind, can't I?' he'd say. 'Sure, but you have to tell me.' Then he'd finally mount the horse and take off. I think he was a manic-depressive."

"'Bipolar disorder' is more acceptable these days." Jury smiled.

Stewert laughed. "Whatever you want to call it, he had it. The thing is, some days he was different, even sunny, you could say. Took any horse I saddled up. Funny, but he rode better on those days. Mounted better."

"I expect you can do anything a little better if you feel better."

Stewert didn't reply. He was staring at the wall behind Jury. "I need to clean that shotgun."

"Shotgun?" It was hanging on the wall Stewert was staring at.

"Oh, she's a shooter. Didn't you know?"

"I didn't, no. How are the Treadnors to work for?"

"Well, like I said, you never could tell about Tom; he was, I guess you'd say, moody. I never knew how I'd find him when he came out of the stable. Hot and cold. But she's okay. It's a good job. Good-paying. Will need to find a new stable master."

"I might know someone. Thank you very much, Mr. Stewert. You've been a lot of help."

Jury shook his hand and left the stable, rather sad to go. The horses, he'd found, were a kind of comfort.

Reluctant to leave the grounds, he sat down on a wooden bench facing a tall hedge that seemed to run the length of the house.

# 13

What hit him first was the football.

What hit him second was the dog.

The football, thought Jury, was probably an unsuccessful kick or pass.

The dog wasn't. He was just there by his elbow on the arm of the bench. The dog stared up at him as if Jury should have done a better job at receiving the ball and maybe passing it back to him.

*Yap, yap, yap.* Pant.

The boy suddenly appeared beside the dog. "He wants you to throw it."

"I guessed that. But isn't it a little big for him to carry?" The dog was a terrier, curly coat and all ears. Jury threw the ball toward the field that lay on the other side of the tall hedge.

The dog took off. The boy, probably seven or eight, kept on looking at Jury. He was a thin lad, and his hair stood straight up in little peaks. He was holding a packet of Doublemint gum.

"What's your dog's name?"

"Gizmo. Bet you never heard that before, right?"

"Yes, I have. That's my sergeant's name."

"*Wot?* People aren't named that!"

"Not many people. But we're police." As if that explained things. Jury flicked a finger at the chewing gum. "Think I could have a stick of that?"

The boy's hair stood up even straighter, a tablet of spikes. The gum was thrust toward Jury, who took a stick.

"Who's your barber?"

By now, Gizmo was back, the end of the football clamped in his mouth. He came to stand by the boy, his head reaching only to the seat of the bench.

"Barber? I don't have a barber."

"What about Gizmo here? Who's his barber?"

Alerted, Gizmo dropped the ball. As if he'd had his fill of barbers too.

The boy looked at the dog, the dog at the boy, as if the two were on the same wavelength: *Who is this crazy guy?* "Dogs don't have barbers!"

"And what's your name, then?"

"Me? Tommy. Tom."

"Well, Tommy-Tom, I'm—"

"No, no, no. Just *one*: Tommy. Tom's my uncle. My . . . main uncle."

"Main? Then who's the secondary one?"

Here came a furious head shake.

Ear shake.

"There's no second. Just him, my main—no, *great*-uncle. Sir Thomas Treadnor. Only he is dead now," Tommy said, looking sorrowful.

"I am sorry, Tommy," said Jury. "He was a knight, was he?"

"No. A lord."

"Really?"

"Of course. He's the greatest!"

"Again, I am sorry, Tommy," Jury said solemnly. "You really liked him, didn't you?"

Tommy flung out his arms. "He is my favorite!" Tommy paused. "Only he thought I shouldn't play football."

"Why not?"

"He kept telling me it's too dangerous. Over and over, he told me. He even hid the football. But I still did it. I'm going to be a famous player."

Gizmo turned his head to stare at Tommy.

"Is Gizmo going to be an even more famous player?"

"Don't be daft!"

Would this craziness never end? Apparently not, for now the tall, crazy man rose, picked up the football, and flung it so far it disappeared across the field.

And that did it. Both of them, arms out, ears out, flung themselves after it. Both disappeared behind the tall hedge and then reappeared, running for all they were worth. Jury watched and chewed gum and was happy. At that moment, Wiggins came and stood beside him, neck stretched, eyes shaded, looking over the field. "Who're the kids?"

"Kid. One kid, one dog. That's Tommy Treadnor, the victim's great-nephew, who's pretty broken up about his death. The dog's Gizmo."

"Gizmo. That's a good name for a dog."

Or detective, Jury didn't add. Wiggins stood thinking until suddenly Tommy and Gizmo burst through the tall hedge.

"Whoa!" said Jury, holding out his arms.

"I won!" called out Tommy. "Got three downs right around him!"

Gizmo glared at Tommy.

"Well, two then," said Tommy.

Jury said, "Tommy, how can you beat a dog in football?"

"You shoulda been watching. Who's this then?"

Jury smiled. "This is Detective Sergeant Wiggins."

Tommy smiled brilliantly. "DS Gizmo Wiggins? How d'ya do?" Tommy put out his hand.

Gizmo Wiggins was not sure what to do with it.

# 14

An hour later, they had left the Treadnor house and were driving at what Jury considered a sullen speed.

"Give it a little more gas, Wiggins, and we might make it to London before that cow."

Wiggins thought of a half dozen possible responses to this but decided none was very good, so he let it pass.

"Ye gods," said Wiggins, "we're practically in the center of London now. What is that herd of sheep doing in the middle of the road?"

Wiggins honked at an old sheepherder or the sheep themselves that seemed planted in the middle of the road ahead. Slowly, the man moved to the side, signaling for the sheep to move also, which they did. "My God, where's he taking the sheep? Sheep convention, maybe?"

"To the Albert Hall, maybe?" Jury looked up at a nearly cloudless sky the color of marble.

"The Royal Albert Hall, sir? That's where they have the BBC Proms."

"Sure. It's a very literal venue." Jury turned to look at him. "I was only kidding, Gizmo."

"I beg your pardon. Gizmo?"

"It's what Tommy Treadnor, the great-nephew, named you."

Wiggins looked genuinely confused. "I don't understand."

"He was only kidding too." Talk about missing the point. "Let's get back to Treadnor, okay?"

"Did you talk to the chef, Santos?"

"Of course. I was in the kitchen."

"What did you get out of him?"

"Only a recipe." Wiggins laughed. "That's it."

Jury sat up smartly. "What? You got a *recipe* out of Santos?"

"Fig spread. He'd made it for Mr. Treadnor to spread on bread or toast. You see, Treadnor hated Nutella, but Tommy was always clamoring for his uncle to eat it with him. So the chef, Santos, says, 'I never liked the stuff'—he meant the fig spread—'but it looked like Nutella, so Mr. T'—that's what Santos called Treadnor—'Mr. T could pass the figs off as Nutella.' The fig spread looked just like it.

"'Nice guy,' Santos said. I think he really liked Treadnor. I told him I thought the fig spread was good, so he gave me the recipe."

*Wiggins gets a recipe, and I couldn't even find out what was for dinner*, thought Jury.

# 15

The rain seemed to stop obligingly just as he reached Boring's front door, so Jury was able to shake off the accumulated drops from his coat before he stepped out of the cab, and it drove away.

Although Boring's was aglow as usual with the burnt light from the cones on either side of the fireplace and the dusty light gathered in the rings of cigar smoke, to Jury it breathed tranquility as he sat down in the Members' Room. He said so.

"Let it breathe as it will," said Melrose, "as long as it pours single malt and Swarovski. God, do I need a drink!"

Jury picked up his brandy, took a drink. "Stewert, the stable man, is leaving. He said they were looking—"

"No."

"No what? You don't know what I was about to say."

"Oh, yes, I do. You're always landing me with your jobs. The last one took me to Kenya. Then there was the North York Moors, where I was the antiques expert. So no thanks. I don't want the stable job."

"Stable master. I told her you were accomplished at it." That was a lie.

"What in hell's a stable *master*?"

"Just what it sounds like." It didn't sound like anything, so Jury amplified. "You'd notice if a horse's coat was, say, too dry. Or undergroomed."

"Undergroomed? I don't even know what overgroomed is."

"*Well*-groomed, you mean. Or if the horse looks unhappier than usual."

"Ye gods, I don't know if *you* look unhappier than usual. And you're human. Or were." Melrose huffed a little and drank his whiskey. "But get this: I absolutely refuse to muck out stables!"

Jury noted that Melrose was setting conditions. He was making progress. "Of course you wouldn't be doing common jobs like that. That would be left to a stable lad."

Melrose looked around as if one were suddenly to appear. None did. "As far as I know, I haven't had one."

"Gerrard."

"*What? Gerrard?*"

"Sure. Take him along. Alice Treadnor was fascinated by all of this." She would have been, had she heard it, thought Jury.

"So am I."

"She thought there was something almost elegant about a master and stable lad."

"And what would Gerrard be doing besides the mucking out?"

"All of the things you don't want to do."

"Which is all of them."

"Dress-wise, just wear your usual thousand-quid jacket and a flat cap."

"No. I refuse to wear a flat cap. I've never worn a flat cap—"

"I don't mean the moth-eaten kind your hermit wears. I mean like a nice tweed one. Get that tailor of yours to sew one up."

"You really don't understand clothes, do you?"

"No," said Jury. "Now, this job."

"No," said Melrose.

"All I said was Rufus Stewert is probably going to quit."

"No. For one thing, I know nothing about horses."

"You've got Aggrieved. Who recently won a stakes race, if you recall."

"Not because of me. Because he was trained by Gerrard Gerrard."

"The stable master's pay is very good."

Melrose heaved a giant sigh. "Look around you: Look at Neame and Champs, sitting by the fire, probably counting trust funds; look at the furnishings; look at the polish, the porters, the people. Does this place look like a hideout for the homeless? Do you think you can lure me with *money*?"

Jury had not been thinking of a lure. But now he did. Perhaps the elegance of Treadnor House? Hardly. Ardry End had just as much, if not more, than Treadnor. Kith and kinship? That was a laugh. There were certainly no kin, and Jury hadn't seen any trace of friendliness. Thus, Jury resorted to the one argument nearly everyone found irresistible: giving up. "Okay, you win."

"What?" Melrose did not want to win by default. "You mean you're just giving up?"

"Yes. You clearly don't want the job. Is there more of this?" Jury held out his glass.

"Did you ever know Boring's to run out? And you just got a drink. That's Bunnahabhain, one of the priciest whiskies *in the world*."

"You can afford it; you don't even need a job." Jury kept his glass out and slid down in his chair. He loved Boring's: the leather, the drinks, the food, the people—everything Melrose had mentioned.

Melrose gestured to Young Higgins, who appeared with a suddenness that was akin to a leap, considering his age, which Melrose thought was 110. "Could we have two more, Higgins?"

Higgins turned with his tray, and Melrose added, "What's on the menu tonight?"

"I believe it's pavés du Mail with either dauphinoise potatoes or a poutine. Thank you, sir." Higgins left.

His French was impeccable, if it was French. Melrose wasn't sure about the Higginsonian French. "What in the hell's that?"

"Meat and potatoes," said Jury.

Melrose was more surprised by this than by Higgins's French. "How in the hell do you know?"

"Just because I'm poor doesn't mean I'm dumb. 'Dauphinoise' means potatoes au gratin. I do not know what 'poutine' is, but I'm assuming it's another form of potato, as we get to pick one. I'm guessing the other thing is meat—fish wouldn't go with potatoes au gratin, would it? And he'd be telling us the entrées. I am a detective, after all. Ah good, here's the booze."

Higgins was back and handing each a fresh glass. Melrose, who was staring at Jury during his menu recitation, said (now wanting to refresh the argument so he could win it with his own cleverness), "I'd have to live in bloody Twickenham; it's too far from Northampton to drive to the Treadnor place every day."

"She'd probably put you up in the house."

"Give the stable man a room? I doubt it. Anyway, you don't expect me to live with someone else, do you? I'm used to a whole house to myself."

"I agree." Jury took another drink of the pricey whiskey. "But you could live in Boring's. This isn't far from Twickenham."

Which is what Melrose was planning to do. "Ah, wouldn't that just drive Agatha insane?"

"Yep." Jury enjoyed his friend's talking himself into this job.

"I certainly have no intention of mucking out stables."

"That's no problem. You could get Gerrard Gerrard to do any stable jobs you don't like."

"Which is all of them."

"When are we going to get the meat and potatoes? I'm starving."

Irritated that Jury was just letting the argument go again, Melrose made another sign to Higgins: "Can we get a table now, Higgins?" Knowing damned well they could get one whenever they wanted.

"Certainly, sir. Right away." Higgins went toward the dining room, where he also put in time as headwaiter.

"Higgins is overworked," said Jury. "Maybe he could get the stable master job."

"Ha ha."

They sat down by one of the beautiful wooden pillars that seemed to act as a curtain for privacy.

"What was that entrée?" said Melrose.

"Something du Mail." Jury thought for a moment. "Probably has to do with the Rue du Mail and some bistro or other."

"My God!" said Melrose. "How do you know that street?"

"I *was* in Paris, if you remember."

"Everybody was in Paris. But they don't recall some café on the Rue du Mail."

"Don't be such a snob. 'Everybody'? There are actually a few people who have never been there. Where's the wine?"

"I haven't ordered it yet. And no, I don't want your advice." Melrose held his hand out.

"I don't know anything about wine; you know that."

"I didn't think you knew anything about the Rue du Mail either. Let's see, a Bordeaux would be swell, if this is indeed beef we're eating."

"Let's take a chance."

"No." Melrose gestured Young Higgins over.

"M'lord."

Melrose was still titled as far as Boring's was concerned. Boring's loved a title.

"Is this entrée some sort of beef?"

"Indeed. It is. It's Wagyu."

"Ah! The best there is."

"Sir," said Higgins, turning on his heel.

"What the hell's 'Wagyu'?" asked Jury.

"You mean you don't know? Japanese beef. It's far more marbled."

Jury sighed. "I'm not going to ask."

"Good."

"Could we go back to the job?" said Jury. "I don't think you have to be there eight hours a day."

"I'm glad to hear it. So I can turn down four hours a day."

"Oh, come on, Melrose. I really need somebody in that house to help out." Jury tried a bit of a wheedle.

"When's he leaving?"

This was progress, Jury thought. "I don't know. I'll find out."

Melrose was consulting the wine list again. "How about a nice Pape Clément?"

"I'd take a nice rubbing alcohol at this point."

Melrose sighed. "It's a Bordeaux."

"Red, huh?"

"Wow! Did you pick that up on the Rue du Mail?"

"Oh, get over it, will you?"

Melrose laughed, getting over it.

# 16

The only horse Melrose had a long-standing relationship with was Aggrieved, a horse that seemed to be barely putting up with him. Whenever Melrose mounted him—or, more precisely, got up on his back somehow—Aggrieved could hardly contain a sigh (or so it seemed to Melrose).

Aggrieved was taken care of by Gerrard, the stable lad, and Mr. Blodgett, Melrose's hermit-in-residence. Melrose had hired him after reading in *Country Life* that all the best people in the eighteenth century had hermits on their property, as people in the twenty-first century might have swimming pools or tennis courts, only hermits served no purpose other than adornment, symbolizing wealth and prestige.

Gerrard Gerrard was, if not a hard worker, extremely clever for a lad of thirteen or fourteen or twelve; that Melrose didn't know his exact age was testimony to Gerrard's cleverness. But his principal value was in his ability to keep his aunt Agatha away from the house. She would occasionally brave his presence if she was desperate either for tea or for more proof that he was really related to Melrose—which she claimed not to believe for a minute. ("That pigheaded little North Londoner? Don't be absurd! Keep in mind your father and mother and his title, fourth Lord Ardry, baron of Ross and Cromarty.")

"You needn't remind me of the title, one I've forgone, as you know. And there were certainly relations outside of that title. Not everyone in Northamptonshire or the surrounding counties had rights to it."

"Don't be ridiculous, Plant. Of course, I know—"

But did she really? She was surprised by Gerrard, wasn't she? "Such as who? You've never mentioned anyone."

He had not bothered mentioning them now, as there was no one. There wasn't Gerrard, either, but he let her stew.

Thus, Gerrard had made himself helpful, hanging about the barn, grooming Aggrieved (who didn't want it—didn't, Melrose bet, think he needed it; the horse was so conceited), and even doing unpleasant work, like mucking out stables. He would also help out Ruthven and his wife Martha, the cook at Ardry End, both of whom he liked exceedingly, often referring to Ruthven as "a card." He'd thought Ruthven to be extremely funny from the first time he'd met him, which seemed strange to Melrose, as he never thought of the butler as a joker even when he, Melrose, was a little kid.

Gerrard also liked Richard Jury, a liking Jury was probably playing on in his attempt to get Melrose to take on the job at Treadnor House.

Melrose couldn't wow Alice Treadnor with his horse experience. She, however, could wow him with her ethereal beauty. No, "ethereal" was not the right word—indeed, neither was "beauty." Her looks were in some ways indescribable.

"Mrs. Treadnor," said Plant. "I'm applying for the stable master job."

"You look overwhelmed, Mr. Plant."

"No, I feel trapped or caught or something like that."

"I'm sorry."

"You didn't do that." This woman's husband had been shot; why was he saying dumb things?

"I suspect I've lost the job."

"No, that's up to Rufus Stewert. I'll have Alan take you to him."

"Alan!" she called.

The stables were at the rear of the house.

Here Melrose said, "You're Mr. Stewert?"

"Just Stewert. You've had experience, Mr. Plant?"

"Absolutely." Melrose thought of Aggrieved.

"Your experience includes thoroughbreds?"

"Absolutely. Yes."

"You've ridden them?"

"No. Except for my own."

Stewert looked puzzled. "You own a thoroughbred?"

Melrose gave him a look that said, "Doesn't everybody? But then I had a stupid accident." Here Melrose patted his knee, which hadn't shown any signs of injury. Now he had to plow on and wound up having a knee replacement. He thought that at least would get him out of any future riding of thoroughbreds.

"I know a stable boy who's coming today. He should be here now. He's great with exercising horses." And if anyone could talk his way into a job, it was Gerrard.

"I'd like to talk to him."

"Of course." Melrose wanted to add, "You'll regret it."

And here Gerrard came along, whistling his way up the path. Melrose hadn't got the chance to pull him aside and tell him this was the man doing the hiring.

The introduction was barely out of Melrose's mouth when Gerrard had his hand out and was saying, "Pleased to meetcha. I had a lot of horse experience before I started working for Lord Ardry—uh, I mean, for Mr. Plant." Before Gerrard could list his every horse accomplishment, Melrose interrupted.

"Yes, Gerrard has always been good with my horse, Aggrieved."

"Good? That there horse won the Sundown Stakes like any thoroughbred."

"So, I hear you keep thoroughbreds?"

Gerrard said, "More'n you can imagine!"

Melrose refused to allow him to maximize Ardry End's stables. "We've only had three." He couldn't bear to say "one," as if Aggrieved wasn't enough.

Stewert looked up at the brass harness he was polishing and said, "You two make quite a team. I'll recommend both of you for these jobs."

# 17

When Jury got off the elevator that morning, he saw Superintendent Racer several doors ahead of him, walking with a broom, not sweeping, but carrying.

He heard the comment flung over his shoulder and into Fiona's office: "Sweep that ball of mange straight to hell, Miss Clingmore! Find him!" Racer kept walking and peering into any open doorways.

When Jury got into his office, he wasn't surprised to see Wiggins drinking tea, but he was surprised to see Cyril sitting on Wiggins's desk with something small and glittery in his mouth. When Jury bent down to inspect it, he found a bejeweled gold cufflink.

Ah! he thought. The broom! Of course, he could have just taken it away from Cyril, but where would be the fun in that?

"Come on," he said, nodding toward Cyril. The cat jumped down and followed Jury out the door and down the hall to Racer's office.

The broom was now coming from the other direction. Jury gave Cyril a little kick to hurry him in. Fiona started to babble, and Jury said, "Later," as he escorted the cat into Racer's office.

At the back of the room, Jury gave Cyril's head a little tap: "Drop it." The cat dropped the cufflink at the rug's edge.

Jury's foot shoved the desk a little just as Racer was coming through the doorway. He still held the broom. Cyril had already swept through the air between the desk and bookshelf, where he lay now.

"Bloody ball of mange," said Racer, stuffing the broom into the umbrella stand.

"Cleaning service didn't show up again?" said Jury.

"Very funny."

Jury, still by the desk, moved his foot slightly and knelt down. "What's this?"

"Where did that come from?" demanded Racer.

"You must have dropped it in your sudden urge to kill the cat. Well, Wiggins and I have to meet somebody in the city, so we'll be going."

"Take that bloody ball of mange with you."

Cyril's tail twitched when Racer rose from his chair as if he was leaving.

Jury was standing now by the umbrella urn. Reaching into it he said, "If I can just use this?"

Racer looked up. "Get the hell out!"

Cyril sprang.

Jury left.

With the broom.

# 18

"You've still heard nothing from Mr. Lederer?" said Jury when he and Wiggins were sitting in the office on Broadchurch Street.

"Not a word," said Davies. "He was going to Cancún, and as far as we know, he went, but Chicago can't get in touch with him. We're still trying."

So are we, Jury didn't say. Neither did Wiggins, after Jury kicked his foot. "I know we went over this before, but I'm asking you again, what did you know about Mr. Lederer?"

"As I said before, Superintendent, absolutely nothing." Davies spread his hands to indicate the nothingness he knew.

"You're assuming I mean big things about his life—family, how he spent his weekends. No, I'm talking about very small things. Were you at a copy machine together? In a business meeting? Both talking to the same person? In the toilet? Anything at all?"

Davies seemed to pull back at the toilet reference but merely said, "Well, of course, I was in contact with Jason from time to time." He sat back and twiddled his thumbs, then looked at them. "He cracked his knuckles—but very consciously, if you know what I mean. It wasn't habitual behavior. Just something he did as if really to check up on his joints, to see if they were tight. Then he'd shake his hands"—Davies did this, to demonstrate—"almost like a tennis player or a golfer might do before picking up a racket or a club. I don't do either, so how would I know?" Davies laughed. "And I don't imagine that's the kind of stuff you want to hear."

"It's exactly the stuff, Mr. Davies. Anything else?"

Davies frowned. "Not offhand, but I'll certainly let you know if I think of something. But wait. You know, the knuckle-cracking could also have had in it an element of nervousness, since he had a few nervous characteristics. Like, he'd cross his leg—you know, as we all do." Here he drew one foot atop his other knee and started fidgeting the foot. "He did that all the time. He was like somebody who had a hard time sitting still." Davies looked at Jury almost expectantly, as if there might be another compliment.

Which Jury was happy to provide. "That's giving us a picture of Mr. Lederer we didn't have before, Mr. Davies. These small things might provide an important key as to what happened."

Davies beamed. Jury really liked the man. There was something in his manner that was full of suppressed little-boy surprise, just waiting to come out.

Jury thought, then asked Davies, "Are there any of your employees here who might be associated with Jason?"

Davies thought about this. He said, "Thumbelina. She's quite acquainted with Jason, I believe." Davies called Thumbelina on the intercom and asked her to come over to his office, which she did.

Thumbelina—a name Jury could hardly get out in one piece without falling on the ground and beating the wooden floor with his fist—was slender, with smooth, chestnut-colored skin, brownish hair, and hazel eyes. She was wearing a dress in a brilliant shade of green, and floated by the reception desk like a summer leaf.

"This is Superintendent Jury and Sergeant Wiggins from New Scotland Yard. They would like to ask you a question or two about Jason," said Davies.

Thumbelina politely nodded her head. She said, "I hardly knew Jason at all. He was not a forthcoming person."

"Did you know anything at all about his family?" asked Jury.

"Only that most of them lived in the United States, but he does have a sister here in London, who lives somewhere in Fulham. I can get the address for you. I'm sure I have it somewhere."

"I appreciate that, Thum-be-li-na." Jury could hardly get the name out.

"Just wait here for a moment." She walked over to a desk, opened the drawer, and took out a Rolodex and a pad of paper. She found the card she was looking for and copied down the information that was on it. She went back to Jury with a scrap of paper.

"Her name was Sally. Her proper name was Sarah, but Jason referred to her as Sally. She does live in Fulham, near Heathrow Airport."

"Is there anything else you can tell us about Jason?"

"From what I can gather, he is quite talented. He plays the piano."

"Does he make money doing it?"

"That I don't know. But I imagine living in Docklands, he'll be making money from it."

Jury thanked Thumbelina as he and Wiggins got up from their seats.

"Thanks, Mr. Davies. We'll be going now."

Before they opened the door to leave, Davies said, "It's been borne out, hasn't it?"

Jury and Wiggins turned. "What?"

"Surprises. Lederer was mysterious. He's gone from Chicago and hasn't turned up in Cancún or anywhere else we know of. That would qualify as surprising." Davies smiled.

"You're right there, Mr. Davies. Thanks."

Davies gave them a little farewell wave.

# 19

When Jury arrived at the Treadnors' house, it was Alan who came to the door. "Superintendent Jury. Was Mrs. Treadnor expecting you?"

"No. But can I talk to her, Mr. Robson?"

"Let me find her for you. She went out for a ride, but she should be back by now. Can I get you tea?"

Jury said, "No, thank you."

By this time, they were in the living room and Alan said, "Have a seat, I'll look for Mrs. Treadnor."

Alice was back after five minutes.

"Mr. Jury, how do you do? Can I offer you a drink? We have gin, brandy, bourbon—just about anything except rum. Tom hated rum."

"Ah, no, thanks."

"Well, I'll start with one of my baroque Manhattans. I'm not trying to get drunk, Superintendent. Takes too much effort." She looked around and said, "If I could just find the damn cherries."

On the intercom she called to someone named Tabby to "bring the real cherries." Just then, Tabby arrived with a small dish of what Jury presumed to be the "real" cherries. He saw Alice hand the jar of maraschinos to the maid—obviously the unreal ones.

"You have to talk to me?"

"About your husband. For one thing, in my questioning of your staff, I found that Tom Treadnor called up many different feelings."

"But doesn't everyone?"

"Call up differing feelings in others, yes, but not in the way he does. Your chef, your cook, your butler—"

"Alan is more a house manager—"

"That's what a butler is. The servant who manages the house, the highest-ranking staff member. But let's not get off the subject again; I'm interested in the variety of feelings Mr. Treadnor called up. Alan Robson, for instance, held him in high esteem—"

"He would do, wouldn't he? Tom gave him a job after Alan had been out of work for five years."

"I'm not talking about dramatic things. And not even about the feelings of different people. Tom Treadnor seemed to make people both like him and dislike him. Your stable man, Stewert, for instance, thought him both self-effacing and egotistical. He was at the same time humble about his poor horsemanship and very difficult to instruct in the right way of doing things, like mount—"

"Oh, people can be different at different times."

Jury paused briefly. Then he said, "Jason Lederer." He had his hand on the folder he'd taken from his trench coat pocket.

"I beg your pardon?" She seemed deeply puzzled.

Jury opened the folder and shoved the picture of Lederer toward her.

She stared at it. "But that's . . . Tom."

"No, it isn't Tom. It's Lederer. You didn't recognize him—or rather, misidentified the victim as your husband."

"Obviously not. The resemblance of the dead man to Tom was extraordinary—as you must have realized, given all the others who made the same mistake. But of course, I don't blame you for being baffled. I am his wife, after all; remember, though, I didn't look very long at the man's face. He'd been sitting in Tom's regular place at the bar. Which was even more peculiar."

"So you think the shooter was going after your husband, and killed the wrong guy? Why would someone want to kill him in such a bizarre way, Alice?"

She looked away from her cocktail shaker. "But did someone?"

"Surely, that's the only way of explaining this, well, 'accident.' "

She said, "I assure you, I've never seen this man who was shot. Never. And shot *through a window*? Good lord, how could that happen?"

Jury then said, "That raises another question, Mrs. Treadnor, about your husband."

Dropping a cherry in the big glass, she turned. "What's that?"

"Where is he?"

# 20

"You said Alice Treadnor can handle a shotgun?" This is what Melrose said to Jury later in Boring's, where they were having dinner in its beautifully paneled dining room and where the special that night was Dover sole, Jury's favorite.

"Exceedingly well, according to her stable man, Stewert."

"But that would be taking a hell of a chance, what with the possibility of people walking by and cars driving by."

"Of course, but it's understood whoever did it would know he or she had to be fast, and also make his or her presence there seem reasonable."

"How?"

"I don't know. I know only that you'd have to be quick and look as if you belonged—"

"Belonged? You mean doing something outside, like trimming the hedges. You wouldn't be doing stuff like that at night, though."

Jury frowned, thinking. "Painting. They were painting the pub."

Melrose laughed. "You wouldn't be doing *that* at night, either."

"According to the owner, they just came round whenever they pleased—a peculiar bunch, but excellent painters. Yes, a couple of them would come by at night, with strong lights. You know, set them on the ground and paint." Jury cut off another bite of sole. "Does this conversation have a point? Because we're out of wine." Jury was lifting an empty bottle from the cooler.

"Oh, for God's sakes. Food, drink. Is that all you think about?" Melrose gestured to Young Higgins, who moved in good-natured decrepitude toward their table. Melrose said to Jury, "Should we have another bottle of the Pouilly-Fuissé?"

"Okay by me. What century?"

Young Higgins removed the offending empty bottle and drifted off.

"That'll probably set me back a hundred quid."

"Probably. You've expensive tastes."

They both decided on queen of puddings for dessert, given the alternative was spotted dick, which Melrose described as "raisin-studded dough."

"How about a dessert wine?" said Jury. He signaled to Young Higgins, who arrived with wings on his heels. Jury ordered something and said, "We barely touched the second bottle of P.F."

"P.F.? That what you call a Latour Puligny-Montrachet?"

"You only know that from reading the label," said Jury.

"And what's this that Young Higgins has had to climb down to the cellar to drag up?"

"I don't know. It just looked good."

A voice at Jury's elbow said, "Superintendent Jury! Lord Ardry!"

This enthusiastic greeting was voiced by Colonel Neame, who stood there with Major Champs. Two of Melrose's favorite Boring's denizens.

Young Higgins was back and placing a bottle before Jury.

"Good lord!" said Colonel Neame. "You fellows really know how to drink! That's a 1969 single harvest port. I wouldn't mind a jolt of that myself."

Jury waved his hand. "Please do join us. Care for some dessert?"

Young Higgins was there with the puddings and two more glasses, which he distributed. "Shall I pour, sir?" This was addressed to Melrose, even though Jury had ordered the wine. Young Higgins knew which side his bread was buttered on.

"Please do."

"And you, Superintendent? Find another questionable corpse in Boring's?" asked Major Champs between a sputter and a cough.

"Are corpses ever questionable, Major?" said Jury with a laugh.

"I would say so," said the major. Then, going on in a whispery voice, he said, "After one of the maids went down—plunk!—in a bedroom, it was discovered she had rooms in Blackwell Gardens.

"Well, *that's* a bit rich!" said Colonel Neame. "I hadn't heard that, Champs. You keep your ear to the ground. Delicious, Lord Ardry! Thank you!" He raised his glass in a salute.

"Oh, don't thank me, Colonel. Thank our connoisseur, Mr. Jury. His choice."

Neame raised his glass again, this time to Jury, and Champs regarded the desserts that Higgins had brought.

"Ah!" said Champs. "I see that you plumped for the pudding. Wanted to myself but thought it was too rich after that sole. Dover sole's a rich fish."

"It certainly is," said Melrose, starting in on his dessert. "Care for some?" he said to the two guests.

"No, no," said Colonel Neame. Then he rose, with Champs soon following. "Better get back to the Members' Room and leave you two to finish your dinner."

Both of them left, giving a small salute.

Seeing that Jury wasn't really eating, but fiddling with a fork, Melrose said, "Something wrong? You've been looking very thoughtful."

Jury shook his head. "No. I've just been trying to remember something they said. One of them. It snagged as it went by and now I can't fix it."

Melrose looked thoughtful. "About the Puligny-Montrachet, maybe? Or the crack about the 'questionable corpse'?"

Again, Jury shook his head.

"The maid! The maid of easy virtue who toppled onto the carpet?"

Jury thought for a moment. "No. Not the maid. For some reason, whatever it was made me think of the Red Queen."

"I'd think *anything* these days would make you think of the Red Queen. What? Why are you getting up?"

"I just remembered I promised Carole-anne I'd buy her a present. Sorry, I've got to go. Very rude of me."

"True, but I'm used to it."

Jury turned. "What's that supposed to mean?"

Melrose laughed.

# 21

Inside, he stood in front of the resplendent assortment of chocolates in their glass cases, wondering if Carole-anne liked chocolate. Was he kidding? She liked any food that was not good for her, which meant ignoring the close-by produce department. Jury marveled that a shop like Fortnum's would sell oranges and pears. Jewel-like, and as pricey as. The ground floor was veritably a ritzy grocery store.

Jury had always liked Fortnum & Mason. He liked the things he could not buy. He liked all these people with whom he could not socialize. He liked being in Fortnum's and at the same time feeling he did not belong there. Harrods might be equally expensive, but it was so huge and so stuffed with customers that he was sure there were others like himself, so he belonged as much as anyone. But in Fortnum's he was isolated, left out, and for some reason, he liked the feeling.

He watched as a customer pulled down an F&M bag and filled it partway with apples.

"Phyllis?" said Jury. Beautifully rosy, but you could buy just as rosy at Waitrose. Still, if you have the money, why not buy your groceries at Fortnum's. "You often shop here for groceries?"

"Me? I usually go to Safeway."

"Good God, Phyllis. How could you lower yourself?"

"I have had a lot of practice lowering myself, but certainly I've never been upper-class enough to buy my groceries at Fortnum & Mason's. Somehow, I wouldn't think that's why you're really here."

"You'd be right. I'm really here to buy Carole-anne a present."

"You're being ironic. Except you don't buy your own, then? You have staff do it." Phyllis had money but no staff. At least as far as Jury knew, she had no staff. It occurred to him that in all the years he had known her, he had never been to her place. He said this. "I've never been to your city house. Country house? Estate?"

"Flat. Of course, it is very ostentatious. For God's sake, Fortnum's has really got under your skin, hasn't it? The only reason you have not been to my flat is that I prefer yours."

"Because I'm in it?"

"No. Because it is so wonderfully lower-middle-class. Or more middle-middle, as it is in Islington. You're on your way!"

"I'm sorry it's not Knightsbridge."

"I'm glad it's not Newnham. Or where was it that research doctor lived? Mackey?" She smiled. "McAllister."

"Talk about living beneath your means. Wasn't he with Doctors Without Borders?"

"No. His own private version. What a man!"

Jury frowned. "Do you ever say that about me?"

"No. What a police officer, maybe. What an unself-regarding person."

"Me?"

"No. Dr. McAllister. I bet he wouldn't be caught within a mile of Fortnum's."

"Well, me neither. Except for feeling un-at-home."

She went on: "Dr. McAllister is rich, tall, handsome, and selfless. You are the same except for the rich and selfless part."

"Thanks so much."

Phyllis laughed. "What did you get her? Carole-anne. The love of your life."

"For God's sake. She is not the love of my life!"

"Yet you just got her a present for an anniversary that does not exist. You made one up. Just to get her a present."

"She needs presents."

"And I don't?"

"You are rich. She's poor. You've got plenty of presents."

"I do? What did you get her?"

"A bed jacket."

"My! That is quite intimate."

"She said she wanted one."

"What's it like?"

"Oh, furry."

"Furry *how*? Mink-y? Sable-y? Persian lamb–y?"

"*No*. Just something, you know, soft and fluffy. I cannot remember what it's called."

"Angora, perhaps?"

"Yes. But the lining is satin or something satiny, with little dogs cavorting all over it, which is why I bought it. Carole-anne likes dogs."

Phyllis smiled fondly. "That is very sweet. Taking so much trouble picking out a gift. Few people do."

"Then why buy one? I mean, if you are not going to take trouble doing it. I do not ordinarily shop in Fortnum's, obviously, but I really like hanging around it—"

"A CID superintendent has time for such hanging around?"

"—because I like to look at all the stuff I cannot buy. And all the people so high up in the social heavens I'll never interact with. And the feeling I do not belong."

"You like not belonging?"

"In Fortnum & Mason, yes."

"How strange. Most people hate feeling they do not belong."

"But I feel like I do belong on the streets of London, or in New Scotland Yard, or my Islington digs. It's refreshing to be in the prodigious splendor of Fortnum's, knowing I can't buy things and don't belong there. It's like being a kid on a curb, watching some dazzling parade I can't join and consequently do not want to."

Phyllis had put her chin in her hands and was gazing at him. "What's wrong?"

"Nothing is wrong. That is a wonderful capsule description of you. Your lack of self-regard."

He frowned. "I'm self-regarding."

"No, you aren't."

# 22

Melrose was reflecting upon his presence at the Treadnors' house when his reflections were broken into, not by Mr. Stewert but by a small, angry-looking dog that stood and stared—no, glared—at him. Melrose had never had a way with animals, nor with children, for that matter.

Which was too bad, for there was a child right on the heels of the dog. "See, you've found Gizmo. I been looking for him."

"I didn't find him; he found me. He doesn't seem to be too happy about it either way."

"Oh, Gizmo's just like that."

"'Gizmo'? That his name?"

"Yeah. Mine's Tommy."

"And mine's Melrose. How do you do?" He put his hand out to Gizmo.

"You shake hands with *dogs*?"

"Why not?"

The question was rhetorical, but Tommy answered it: "Dogs don't shake hands."

Here was a literal lad. "He seems to like horses if not people." He nodded toward the dog's brief barks at the first horse.

"Who're you, then?"

"'Me, then' is the stable master."

"What's that?"

The eternal question. "A person who oversees the stables."

"Like Stewert?"

"Higher up. If Stewert kept working here, I'd oversee him. As I'll oversee Gizmo."

Tommy laughed and slapped his leg. He'd sat down on a milking stool. "Not likely." He reached into his shirt pocket, either for a gun or a cigarette, thought Melrose. He pulled out a pack of gum.

"Tommy? Then you're the nephew of Thomas Treadnor—I'm sorry about your uncle."

"Me, too. Great-uncle."

The boy looked genuinely upset. "This must be very hard for you. You live here, Tommy, do you?"

"Yeah. Nearly all my life. Uncle Tom was my favorite." He was looking at the ground, poking the stick about, drawing nothing. "What's a stable master do?"

"Almost nothing. Most of the work's done by a stable lad."

Tommy looked around. "Where is he?"

"He's not come yet."

"How old is he?"

"Oh, a little older than you." A little older than everyone, if age were to be measured by street life, not chronology.

"What's his name?"

"Gerrard."

"*Gerrard?* That's a fancy name."

"So is Gizmo." Melrose looked around. "Where is Gizmo?"

"Down there, talking to Razz."

"Razz?"

"Short for Razzamatazz. You know." Here Tommy flexed his fingers and rolled them along as if he were playing piano. "Playing razzamatazz, the old piano roll blues," he sang. "Uncle Tom's favorite song. He played the piano."

"I heard. In a trio, too."

"Yeah, the other ones were Brad and Oscar. Brad plays the cello, and Oscar plays the clarinet *and* the saxophone, if you can imagine that!"

"I can't imagine playing anything but Twenty-One."

"What's that?"

"What I lose my money on. Cards."

"Well, Uncle Tom and those guys even made a record. But they weren't famous." Tommy sounded disappointed.

"Lucky them."

"Huh?"

"Don't be famous, if that's what you're thinking. People won't leave you alone. They all want something. Your signature, your money, your horses, your dog."

"You mean somebody'd want Gizmo?"

Melrose couldn't imagine. But apparently Gizmo could, for he ran over to join in on the conversation. The talk with the horse didn't seem to have provided anger management. He still looked peeved at Melrose.

"I wish you'd told Uncle Tom all that about being famous; he wanted to play in the trio for a living."

That didn't sound at all like the Treadnor Melrose had heard about. "Your uncle didn't like his work?"

Tommy shook his head. "It was just about shoving money around, he said."

Right then, Stewert entered and said, "Well, Tommy introducing you to the horses, is he?"

"No," said Melrose with a smile, "but Gizmo's doing a good job."

Stewert laughed.

"He's a stable master," said Tommy.

"Oh, yeah? You could say I am too."

Tommy opened his mouth, but Melrose spoke to shut him up. "Tommy wanted to know what one did, and I told him he should know from watching you."

Tommy opened his mouth again.

Melrose spoke again: "I'm very sorry about your boss. That must have been an awful shock."

"'Twas," said Stewert. "But, well, he took a lot of chances."

Tommy said, "What d'ya mean? Uncle Tom didn't believe in doing that. He was always telling me—"

"Tommy, don't you need to take Gizmo in for his dinner?"

Gizmo seemed to think so, for he barked and turned in circles.

Tommy, albeit reluctantly, called him away.

When they'd gone, Melrose said, "Tommy seems to think all his uncle wanted to do was play piano in that trio of his."

"That's rich," said Stewert. "The man liked it for a hobby, you might say, but his main interest in life was making money."

"You know, it's strange how a man can make so many different impressions."

Stewert laughed again. "As far as playing in the trio goes, you should talk to his partner—you know, Ross. Ross plays the cello. He's good."

Just then a call came from outside, a woman's voice.

"That'd be Elsie," said Stewert.

"The cook?"

"Probably about lunch. She'd be calling you, I expect."

"Mr. Plant! Would you like a bit of lunch?"

When he came over to where she was standing on the lower step, she went on. With her voice lowered to nearly a whisper, as if she didn't want to give anything away, she said, "Mr. Santos has made a cassoulet, and I assure you it's very good."

"Anything Mr. Santos does needs no assurance. Thank you. Is it ready now?"

"Now, yes, indeed. It's simmering on the stove."

"Well, see it doesn't unsimmer, Mrs. Bloom, before I eat it."

As she laughed, he followed her in.

The cassoulet was comprised of beans, sausage, and duck—or was it chicken?—and definitely was not unsimmered.

"Good, huh?" said Tommy, who was sitting across the table from Melrose, having settled Gizmo underneath with, probably, his own cassoulet.

" 'Good, huh' doesn't really get at it. 'Divine' is more likely to capture the taste."

"Gizmo agrees."

Gizmo had woofed in his opinion.

"Hear that, Mr. Santos? Probably your most demanding food critic."

Santos laughed. "Gizmo likes his bit of sausage."

"Good grief, Mr. Santos. I like my bit too. With my bit of duck and my bit of beans. This is a cassoulet, isn't it? Smells like duck, pork, and sausage in a vast panoply of vegetables and spices."

"Most people have no idea of what's in a French cassoulet."

"Most people have no idea of what's in France."

Santos laughed again. "Sounds as if you've wide-ranging knowledge of it, Mr. Plant."

He'd better be careful that he didn't sound too wide-ranging. But then, didn't they know he was educated? Hadn't Jury made that clear to Alice Treadnor? "No, not at all. Been to Paris once or twice, like everyone." That sounded appropriately snobbish, since everyone hadn't.

"My favorite place," said Santos, taking on some of Melrose's snobbishness for himself.

Tommy was looking at the cassoulet. "It was Uncle Tom's favorite food," he said tearfully.

"Now, Tommy," said Elsie, putting her arm around him, "don't upset yourself, dearie."

"It was," said Santos, looking sad.

Why, then, had he made it, Melrose wondered. "I'm terribly sorry about your uncle."

Tommy went on: "There've been police all over the place."

"Have they discovered anything helpful?"

Santos looked at him. "But that detective—that Scotland Yard man—isn't he a friend of yours?"

Oh, hell. He should be more careful. "Not exactly. An old acquaintance, more. And certainly not likely to give me any information. But it's so elaborate for lunch. I'm used to soup and salad or a sandwich, when I eat lunch at all. I hope you're also serving this for dinner."

"No. Dinner's different." Santos continued with his knife-wielding artistry.

"What will it be?"

Said Elsie, "He won't tell you. He never tells anyone, including the mistress. She keeps trying to find out, but it's no use. She even got that Scotland Yard detective to try."

Melrose was astonished. "She didn't!"

"Ah, but she did," said Elsie.

"And did he?"

"No," said Santos.

"All he could do was remember the things Santos took out of the fridge and the cupboard. It's a game. Like two kiddies, you ask me."

"Uncle Tom could find out. Once when you were making ostrich bucket, and when you made poor steak."

Santos laughed. "Two of my favorite dishes!"

The "poor steak," Melrose figured, was steak au poivre. But he couldn't sort the ostrich.

# 23

Alice was sitting in the living room when Melrose walked through the French doors.

"Hello, Mrs. Treadnor."

She turned on the couch and said, "Hello, Mr. Plant. Are things going well?"

"Getting on extremely well, thanks. And I must compliment you on your chef. I think I just ate the best lunch I've ever eaten in my life. I asked him if he was going to serve the same thing for dinner."

"Oh, he is good, isn't he? Did he tell you? I mean, what he was going to serve for dinner?" She asked this over-casually, as she lit a cigarette.

Nice try, Alice, thought Melrose. Assuming the new guy wouldn't know about this prohibition.

"No. Only that it wasn't what we were eating for lunch." Melrose laughed artificially. "Although he did hint that—" No, he hadn't hinted. But Melrose couldn't resist.

"Yes? Yes?" She leaned over the back of the couch as if this would bring her closer to the dinner menu.

Melrose felt like a rat. "Just something about truffles. A truffled something," he repeated, rattily.

"Truffled . . . What could that be?" She wasn't asking him, merely diving into her catalog of past Santos dinners.

"Well, there's mashed potatoes. I've had them with truffles. Mushroom quiche, perhaps." He could have gone on and on, making up things.

"Oh, I'm sure Santos wouldn't bother with truffle mashed potatoes." She paused, considering. "He said nothing else?"

Wow. Talk about wanting to get to the bottom of something. "Not that I remember, no."

She brightened. Probably, thought Melrose, with an idea. "The thing is, I've lately developed a sort of allergy to certain, uh, spices. It's very peculiar. I can't, for instance, eat anything with cardamom in it. So I wonder if he might have mentioned any dish . . ." She shrugged.

Melrose pretended to think about cardamom, something he knew zero about, and then remembered a soup his cook Martha had talked about. "My cook— I mean, a cook my mother used to have once made a Moroccan soup with cardamom." So what? What did Alice care about his mother's cook?

She didn't. "I was just curious . . . you know, as he thinks up such excellent dishes. It's just that this allergy—"

"Doesn't Santos know about it?" Meanie. He felt like stepping on his own foot.

"No. I haven't mentioned it."

"Would you like me to get—"

"No, no, no. I wouldn't want anyone saying anything because . . . I don't want Santos to think I'm in any way criticizing him . . . you know."

But he's your chef, for God's sakes. Criticize away!

Melrose just stood there, his eyes searching for vacant space, wishing he had his flat cap to turn in his hands. He didn't know how to cut and run. Did employees normally help themselves to an exit? "Well, Mrs. Treadnor, if there's nothing else . . ."

"What? Oh, no. No. Thank you. If there's anything you need, I'm sure Alan can see to it."

"I'll be off, then." Melrose turned away.

"Yes, Alan told me you wouldn't be staying with us. Where are you staying?"

"With someone I know in London."

"But that's a bit of a trip every day, isn't it?"

"I'm used to it," he said, meaninglessly, and bowed and turned, then turned back. "Speaking of your chef, Mrs. Treadnor, did he ever mention an ostrich dish?"

"*Ostrich?* Good lord, no. Why? Did he say anything—"

"No, no. I must have misunderstood. Well, I'll get back to the stables, then."

"And has your stable lad arrived yet?"

Speak of the devil. Gerrard was at that moment walking through the French doors.

"And this," said Melrose, "is Gerrard."

Gerrard stepped up smartly with hand extended. "Gerrard Gerrard," he said. "Pleasure."

Alice shook his hand and said, "I've heard a lot about you, Gerrard Gerrard."

"All of it good, I hope."

Melrose sighed heavily.

Looking around the room, Gerrard said, "Some place!" with a whistle. "I got shown around by some butler or other."

"That's Alan," said Alice. "He's not exactly a butler, he's more a servant of all trades."

"Me being a stable boy," said Gerrard, "I guess I'm pretty much beneath him."

As far as Melrose could tell, Alan considered everybody pretty much beneath him.

Gerrard went on: "This here room is really elegant. Just look at this wallpaper and look at them paintings." He swept his arm around as if he were reintroducing Alice to her own house.

Melrose said, "I've never known you to show that much enthusiasm over Ardry End."

"Yeah, but you only got the one horse."

"Aggrieved won the Somerset Stakes."

"That isn't exactly the Derby or the St. Leger, is it? And it was a walkover, anyway."

"Stop minimizing Aggrieved's accomplishments."

Melrose could tell Gerrard was ready to give Alice a lecture in horse racing, so he pulled his arm and said, "Speaking of horses, we'd better get out to the stables to see Mr. Rufus Stewert."

# 24

But Stewert was not there.

Gerrard leaned over Razzamatazz's stall door, regarding him. The horse appeared to be doing the same thing. They were regarding one another in what seemed to be kinship.

Melrose wondered at this Gerrard-horse affinity. "Did you ever have a horse when you were a kid?" As if he weren't one now.

"Oh, sure, all of us kids had our own horses." He was referring Melrose to his bountiful North London upbringing.

"No need for sarcasm. I was only suggesting you have a way with horses."

"Who's taking care of this lot?" Meaning the horses. "Who's watching over it."

"Me," said Melrose.

"Ha! That's like saying the wind is watching over the water."

"What's *that* supposed to mean?"

"Dunno," said Gerrard. "Just came to me. So what do I do with this lot?" He was looking back and forth along the line of four stalls.

"Same as you do with my lot. Groom, feed, et cetera."

"'Et cetera' meaning muck out, I guess."

"Right."

"What do they pay for all this?"

"'They' do not pay you. I do. You are on my team."

"So is it four times what I get for Aggrieved?"

"You forget, I am not paying you to take care of Aggrieved. I hired you to keep Agatha out of the house as much as possible."

Gerrard grinned. "She really thinks I am a kind of cousin. Or that my da is. She's really afraid, 'There goes the fortune!' But how come you're here working as a stable hand."

"Master, thank you. Because Superintendent Jury needs a spy on the premises. He needs information."

Gerrard approved of Jury. "You mean there's been a murder here?" he asked, hopefully.

"Not right here. In a pub in Twickenham."

"Oh, well. Twickenham. No wonder." He had pulled some sugar cubes from his pocket and was unwrapping them.

"'Oh, well, Twickenham'? As if Twickenham were the murder capital of the U.K.!"

Gerrard snorted. "Nearly. The Guinness, the Quilter. Bloody noses all round."

"They're that soccer-aggressive?"

"In Twickenham? Fist in your face as you walk out the door."

"Hah. Let me have a couple of those cubes. Are you always horse-prepared?"

"It can't hurt." Gerrard dug out a few more sugar cubes, handed them to Melrose. "Unwrap them."

"I'd never have worked that out." Melrose held out the cubes to Razz, who ignored them.

"So who got killed?" Gerrard held out two cubes. The horse gobbled them out of his hand.

"Man who owned this estate. Thomas Treadnor. He was shot in the back while he was sitting at the bar." Melrose frowned at the horse.

"But how could someone do that and no one see it?"

Melrose shrugged. "It was a shotgun."

"For God's sake. How can you take a shotgun into a pub and no one notice?"

"The theory is, the person might not have gone *into* the pub." Melrose unwrapped two more cubes and held them under Razz's nose.

"Done it from *outside*?"

"Right." The horse ignored the cubes. Had he no attraction for animals?

"The whole thing sounds kinda dodgy to me. Is that the reason we're here?"

"Yes. It is the dodginess."

"It doesn't sound—I dunno—quite real."

Melrose thought about this. No, it didn't sound quite real.

# 25

After Carole-anne's too-filling version of French toast, pretty much like her fried bread, Jury spent another filling hour in his office. He was surprised not to see Wiggins, who was always there on his hard office chair, always before Jury, but also surprised to see Cyril sitting on the edge of Wiggins's desk. Jury wondered if Cyril missed Wiggins. No. The reason for Cyril's sitting there seemed to be something on the desk itself. At that moment, Wiggins's phone rang. Jury looked at Cyril. "Well, it's obviously for you. Aren't you going to pick up?" Cyril just blinked.

Jury picked up the phone and was surprised to hear Wiggins sounding a little overwhelmed.

"Something wrong?"

"Yes. I won't be coming in today, boss."

"What's the matter?"

"I just got a call from me mum in Manchester. She's in a terrible state."

"I'm sorry to hear that, Wiggins. What's wrong?"

"You remember I told you once a while back about my sister, BJ. We haven't heard from BJ for years. Mum just got a postcard from her. Apparently from Cornwall."

"Hold it, Wiggins. You told me your sister was dead."

"Yes. I know I did, sir. I'm sorry. I'm certainly not sorry she isn't dead. I'm sorry I told you that. It was something we were just assuming, because no one in the family had heard from her for five years."

"Wiggins, have you forgotten you're a cop, and so am I? We don't go around assuming people are dead."

"Yes, boss. You're right. It was a terrible mistake."

Jury sighed. "So go ahead, Wiggins. What happened?"

"She sent Mum this postcard that showed a picture of Cornwall on the front, but the postmark on the back was so smeared it was almost totally obliterated, so we don't know what part of Cornwall it's from."

"You actually don't know if it is from Cornwall at all, Wiggins. That's something to be determined."

"You see. I can't really explain very well until I get to Manchester and see me mum."

"Of course, Wiggins. Take as long as you need. I hope your mother will be all right, and your sister is okay."

"Would you mind, sir, taking care of this leave request with the guv'nor."

"Of course. I'll run this by Racer if you stop calling him the guv'nor. How long do you think you'll be gone?"

"That's hard to say, sir; depends on what I have to do. I might have to somehow or other search for her."

"It sounds complicated enough, so I shouldn't add to it, Wiggins. Just let me know somewhere along the way what's going on and what I can do."

"Thank you so much, sir. I appreciate it." Wiggins rang off.

Jury and Cyril, leaving the ghost of Wiggins in his office, followed the broom down the corridor. The broom stopped at one door and then the next, receiving a few uncalled-for epithets for his trouble.

"Never mind! Never mind!" said Racer. "This place is festooned with mice, and I'm going to get them."

Festooned with mice? thought Jury. He would work on that coupling of words whenever he got a little free time, which might be sometime soon considering Racer's advance on his own office. He checked the doorways and kept going.

"Good morning," said Fiona Clingmore.

"What's good about it?" said Racer. "Can't you get that rat chaser, rat catcher to do what he's supposed to be doing?"

"If you're talking about Cyril, I don't know what he's supposed to be doing?"

"He's supposed to be catching mice."

"I haven't seen any," said Fiona.

"Well, I saw one. I'm sure it came in here." Racer turned into his office, plunked the broom in the umbrella stand, and stood there heaving with frustration. Jury followed him in, Cyril close behind him. Fiona saw Cyril and started to say something, but Jury interrupted.

"No, Fiona. That's all right. If there's a mouse, either your boss or Cyril will get it."

"Where's Wiggins?" said Racer. "I haven't seen him snuffling up the corridors in at least half a day."

"Wiggins has a family emergency. He had to go to Manchester."

"Wiggins *is* a family emergency. Is he coming back anytime soon?"

"Of course. Though I can't tell you the exact time, since emergencies are not given to exact times."

Racer apparently was very doubtful about this particular family emergency. He kept looking around the room, perhaps thinking that Wiggins would appear from behind one of the bookcases. Oh no, thought Jury. How could he be so wrong? Racer wasn't looking for Wiggins. He was looking for his own emergency. The cat, Cyril, very well might pop out from around, behind, or on top of the bookcase, and Jury noticed Racer's eyes were trained on the umbrella stand.

Racer said, "Is that ball of mange—"

"Which particular ball of mange are you speaking of, sir?"

"Don't get smart with me, Jury. Look over there at the umbrella stand."

That's where Jury was looking, and for a moment, the dark-yellowish knob sticking out from the stand did indeed look like it could have been a small head, but what kind of head it could be was debatable. Certainly, a smooth, round head, but expressionless. It couldn't be Cyril.

He said this to Racer: "That isn't him."

Jury went back to his office and straightened up his desk, which consisted of balling up Racer's last memo and tossing it into the trash. He thought about Bygones, and the impossibly named Thumbelina, and that of course led him to what she'd told him: Lederer's sister, Sally. He knew he wanted to talk to her, but he didn't know when. Well, there's no time like the present. Why not now? He considered this for one minute. Put on his coat. Picked up his keys. And left.

# 26

The narrow little house she lived in was in the cramped confusion of the suburbs of Fulham near Heathrow Airport. Jury walked up the stone path and rang the doorbell. There was a click, and he tried the front door, which swung inward. To the right, there was a row of metal mailboxes. He looked along the row until he saw the name Lederer. He assumed that "S." stood for Sarah, or Sally. He rang the bell. He heard the *flip-flop* he presumed was bedroom slippers, and soon a young woman was standing at the bottom of the steps. She reminded him in a way of the stylist from Pigtails who did Melrose Plant's hair. Indeed, she might have been that young woman, except for her leg, which seemed to be stiff and sore from an old injury that made it hard for her to move it. Her hair was gossamer. Indeed, the whole of her looked gossamer. She was extremely pretty, and her expression was welcoming, despite there being no reason for her to welcome him. He introduced himself and watched her be surprised that Scotland Yard was standing at her letter box.

"I am Sally Lederer. What can I do for you?"

He showed his ID card and asked if she had time to speak with him. Sally said, "Come on upstairs. It's the second floor, and you have to walk."

"That's usually the way it is with second floors," said Jury. They walked up the stairs and turned the corner, walked up another flight, and then they were at her apartment door. At least the apartment itself was a little better lit and brighter than the rest of the building, which was quite gloomy and gave the impression that visitors were not welcome. But Sally was welcoming.

She stood before him holding the bunch of still-raffled clothes she had taken from the defective washing machine. A very shaggy dog came to sit at her feet. The dog, looking as if it could do with the ministrations of Pigtail's salon, did nothing but stare up at Jury until it decided to get a little more active. It started circling Jury's leg. It went around three times in one direction, changed its course, and went three times the other way. Then, apparently tired of that, it decided to climb Jury's leg, taking it for a small tree trunk.

"Stop that," said Sally. The dog stopped only because it couldn't get any farther. Sally then introduced her dog: "This is Slipshod," she said.

"Slipshod is your dog?"

"Yes. He might not look like much, but he is very loyal in a slipshod way."

At that moment, an image of Carole-anne rose before him, and he quickly batted it away.

As if trying to prove his loyalty, Slipshod went over to Jury and tried to climb his leg again. Sally reached down and put Slipshod away. The dog went over to the sofa, and instead of jumping up on it, he tried to climb it—though there was nothing to climb.

"Please sit down, Superintendent. I will get you some tea."

He started to say don't bother, but he remembered tea did not appear to be a bother to anyone. Certainly not to anyone who offered it. So he sat down and did not offer to help, but just slumped in the chair, and the dog crawled up and slumped beside him. Sally turned and saw this. She said, "Come on, get down from there." The dog paid no attention and just lay stretched right next to Jury's leg.

"So, you own the entire building?"

"I do."

"Well, you must have a pretty decent job if you can afford this."

"Oh, it has nothing to do with my job. This is part of the estate. This is the part I got."

"Estate?"

"Yes, when my mother died, the estate was divided between my brother and me. Jason of course got the lion's share, and the lion shares most of it in the U.S."

"And now that Jason is . . ."

"Dead?" she finished for him.

"Yes. Even that is a bit of a puzzle."

"Most of the estate involves property, a large part of which is in the American West or Southwest. There is, if you can believe it, a dude ranch."

Jury laughed. "I get the impression you don't make much use of it?"

"No. However, it does have a manager, and we make quite a bit of money, because Americans, especially those who live in places like New York and Chicago, like to go West and love things like dude ranches. I rarely get there. Jason gets a big kick out of it."

"Sally, what did you think of the shooting in the Queen pub?"

"Certainly that it was shocking. If you are asking me, did Jason have enemies or did he know anyone who might have done that . . . Jason did have enemies. He is what you over here might call a rotter. What we call it in the U.S. is a sick son of a bitch."

Jury sat back suddenly. He had not noticed that the dog had gathered himself up and sat behind Jury's back; he let out a yelp when Jury's weight fell against him.

"Tell me more about your brother."

"Jason was a con artist. He didn't give a damn about other people's suffering."

"Including yours, Sally? I assume that leg is causing you a great deal of suffering."

"You get used to some things."

"No, you don't."

The kettle in the kitchen made a screeching noise as if it were suffering too. Jury started to get up. "I take it the cups and saucers, cream and sugar, and whatever else we need are nearby."

She said, "Yes, they are, and there is a tray on top of the cabinet. Just get that down, put all the stuff on it, and carry it right in here. Thanks very much."

Jury came back from the kitchen with a laden tray—teapot, cups, cream and sugar, and a plate of biscuits the dog was trying to pull off the tray until Sally pushed him down.

Jury went back to his questioning. "You have no idea who was involved in that shooting in the Queen?"

"No."

Jury handed her a cup of tea, to which she added a small amount of milk and a sugar cube, then she thanked Jury.

"What did you think it was?" she added.

Jury drank some of his own tea, looked at it for a moment, and said, "A scheme, but I haven't figured out what the scheme was."

"You haven't? A detective superintendent? You haven't come up with anything?"

"Not yet. In addition to this house, what else did you get from your family's fortune?"

"Nothing else."

"You mean your brother got it all? He didn't divide up what he got with you?"

"No, he didn't."

"I would imagine he got quite a bit of cash, or if not cash, he obviously got things he could have converted to cash that he could have given to you. For example, what can you do about that leg?"

"Surgery," she said.

"Why aren't you getting the money to take care of it?"

"I told you, Superintendent; my brother was selfish."

"Could you have taken him to court?"

"Believe me, Jason was careful about his inheritance. He made sure there were no loopholes. No tears in the legal fabric that would have allowed me to go after him."

Jury thought about this. "Have you talked to a lawyer about this?"

"Yes. Only the one who handled the inheritance."

"You haven't spoken to anybody else?"

"No. I don't know anybody else to speak to about this."

"I do. I'll talk to you later about him." Jury stood up and said, "It was really nice meeting you, Sally. I'm terribly sorry you had such trouble. I am sorry your brother was such a bastard."

"Thank you."

They walked to the door, and Jury went back to his car.

# 27

When Jury drove up, Brad Ross was in the front garden, down on his knees with a trowel amidst some plants Jury didn't recognize from that distance. But then he wouldn't recognize them from closer up, either, knowing nothing about plants, and certainly nothing about planting.

Ross rose when he saw Jury, giving a kind of trowel-wave and calling out, "Superintendent!"

"Mr. Ross! A bit early for the primulas, isn't it?" As if he knew.

Clearly, he didn't. Ross laughed. "Not planting primulas, Mr. Jury. I'm just giving the winter aconite a bit more breathing space." Ross nodded down at a few small clumps of soil.

"When you're done with them, maybe you could do the same for me."

"You don't look like you need more breathing space, Superintendent. However, you might need tea. Or coffee. Or better still, a real drink. Come on in." Ross lodged the trowel in a basket of tools, yanked off his gloves, and started toward the front door. On the steps, he said, "Unfortunately, Eleanor's in London. Getting her Harrods fix."

"That's one thing I can do without," said Jury as they entered the house and walked into the library.

"I couldn't agree more. Now, what'll it be? Cup of tea? Slug of whiskey? I've got some excellent stuff from Treadnor's distillery: Uist single malt. It's wonderful."

"I know. I had a taste of that just last night at a pub with a smashing wine list; their wine expert gave me some. You've got a tremendous whiskey there."

"Right. Only it's not mine. The Treadnor is—was—all Tom's. Uist: I told him, though, not to give it that name. No one can pronounce it unless they're an authority on the Outer Hebrides. And I don't know anyone who's much of one even on the Inner. Usually, people can't get past the Isle of Skye."

"So why did he use that name?"

Ross shrugged. "He thought 'Uist' sounded like 'whiskey.' Let me get you some, instead of talking about it." He turned and turned back: "Or are you on duty and therefore—"

"People keep telling me this isn't my case, so I expect I'm not on duty. Thanks."

"Your reasoning is impeccable." Ross turned to the drinks table and got out two etched-glass tumblers.

Jury could make that out, even if he couldn't tell the difference between tuberose and winter aconite. He accepted the glass from Ross, and they sat down.

"But he hated rum," said Jury.

"That was one thing about Tom. He could shelve his own likes and dislikes for something more important."

"What would be more important, though, than the production of whiskey?"

Ross laughed. "Are you joking, Mr. Jury? This particular one"—he raised his glass—"was vastly popular, even despite its price. I've never understood that. Maybe the rich are drunker than you and me, to paraphrase Fitzgerald."

Jury didn't know why Ross was separating himself from "the rich." "I know one of the whiskies his wife insisted on for her Manhattans."

"That's the vermouth, not the whiskey, she reveres. She insists on this French stuff."

Jury laughed. "That and the cherries she apparently has her cook marinate. Sounds a bit excessive."

"Alice is no stranger to excess. Do you know about the battle she has going with her chef?"

"Oh, God, yes. She tried to get me to find out what was for dinner."

"Alice gets everyone to do that. And did he tell you?"

"Well, let's just say that is a battle Santos appears to be winning."

Jury changed the subject. "You disagreed with your partner about several things, you said—in particular Land Savers."

"Yes, well, that was such an audacious change of mind, I just couldn't understand it. More like land-grabbing than -saving. Done for profit."

"But what if that's not what Treadnor meant? What if he thought this village would really help the disadvantaged?"

"I don't think the disadvantaged would have been able to afford it."

"Affordability was the whole idea, I thought. He left funds in his will to subsidize people who couldn't afford it outright."

"Was that the reason he was killed? To revoke his will? Who would have gained from that?"

"Well, frankly, Mr. Ross, you would have, as administrator of the trust fund."

"So that makes me even more of a suspect."

"No. You have a fairly solid alibi."

Ross sighed and rose, holding up his glass. "I'm having another. You?"

"No, thank you."

"'Fairly solid' says that you think it isn't perfect. My alibi has holes in it, then?"

"No. Say it leaks a little, though."

"The policeman who stopped me was wrong?"

"I doubt that. The police are very good when it comes to times."

"But of course, I was driving to the Queen."

"You could have been driving to hell, Mr. Ross, but if that traffic cop put nine forty-seven on your ticket, it was nine forty-seven all right. So, by that accounting, you couldn't have been at the pub between nine ten and nine thirty, which we know was the time of the shooting. That's a very narrow window, but you weren't looking through it."

"But who on earth would have stopped long enough to climb that ladder and paint a word on the sign?"

"Who said he stopped? He—or she—could have done that earlier."

"In broad daylight? Wouldn't it have attracted more attention?"

"Less, I'd think. A painter on a ladder against a building that's been getting a paint job for a long time? Only fellow painters would have wondered about that."

"Still . . ."

"Yes. We haven't worked that out yet."

"Could we go back to my leaky alibi?"

"Dinner."

Ross was really perplexed here. "Dinner? What about it?"

"You ate before you left. You said you sat down to eat at nine twenty. You recalled that exactly because you'd just finished a phone call with a client in Paris."

"That's right. You can check on that."

"We have. It's not the call; it's that your cook said she was putting dinner on the table right at nine because she had to do something and told you not to be late. But you were. You didn't sit down until nine twenty. What were you doing in those twenty minutes?"

Ross shrugged. "I decided I wanted another drink, that's all. After all, only twenty minutes—"

"As you were leaving the house, she asked you if dinner was all right, and you said, 'Perfect, as always.' But it couldn't have been perfect, since you sat down to it twenty minutes after she put it on the table."

"Well, it might have cooled a little, but—"

"No, Mr. Ross, it would have fallen a little. It was a soufflé. It would have been ruined. So I'm wondering what you were doing during those twenty minutes."

Ross looked dumbfounded. "Why, I was in the living room. As I said, I had another drink."

"I doubt you would have ignored your cook's request just for that."

"What are you suggesting, Superintendent? It certainly sounds as if you suspect me."

"I do. The Queen is a five-minute drive from here. That and five back accounts for ten minutes. In the middle ten minutes you could have been shooting Thomas Treadnor through the window. You're a very good shot."

"Through a window? Into a crowd of customers? You can't be—"

"Serious? But I am. Of course, you wouldn't be shooting into the crowd, but with a clear path to Treadnor's back as he sat at the bar. An extremely difficult shot, yes, but if the trajectory had been impossible, you wouldn't have tried it. You'd just have waited for another opportunity."

"Another opportunity! My God, if I'd wanted to kill Tom, there'd have been myriad opportunities to do it around here. At his house, in the fields—or on a street in the city. To do it the way you're describing doesn't make any goddamned sense!"

"Which is the way your attorney would argue it, certainly, and probably get you off if the prosecutor couldn't come up with something. But the thing is, you're not supplying an alternative as to where you were during that time. Since you weren't eating a soufflé."

Ross looked around the room for something he wasn't finding. "I could have been in the library getting something to read." He shrugged.

"Mr. Ross, please don't play with my mind. You could have been anywhere around here. The question is *where*. Inside? Outside?"

As if Jury had offered him a way out, Ross said, "Yes, now I recall. I stepped out onto the patio to check the Colocasia. The soil looked dry, and I wanted to do a pH test."

"They must be very delicate plants, and the soil must be hard to analyze if it took you twenty-five minutes to check on them. In twenty-five minutes, you could also have gotten in your car, driven somewhere close, driven back."

"Such as where?"

"To the Queen."

"So you think I shot Tom."

"I didn't say that. Only that I'm pretty sure you were there."

"But why would I have been?"

"Maybe to meet somebody who might or might not have shown up."

"Riding that half hour when Hilda was putting dinner on the table?"

"But of course, you wouldn't have known when you made this appointment—if that's what it was—that she would have been serving at that time."

"I don't get it. Why are you so sure I went there?"

"Well, you said you hadn't been in that pub since your partner was shot—"

"That's right."

"And that neither you nor your wife had talked to any extent to Alice, beyond, of course, extending sympathy."

"Right."

"Then how did you know?"

"Know what?"

"That it was now the Red Queen?"

Just then, the door opened, and Eleanor Ross walked in. "Sorry I'm so late," she said, removing her coat and tossing it over the back of a chair. "Harrods was jammed—"

"When isn't it?"

"Oh, Superintendent Jury!"

Jury drove the five—no, six—minutes from the Ross house to the Red Queen, drove into the car park (where he found what was probably the usual number of cars at this pre-six hour), and parked. He got out of his car and walked over to the side window, which the police thought—given the theory the shot was fired from outside—the shooter would have used, and stopped and stared into it for a minute, checking his watch. So far, eight minutes.

"You got business here, mister?" came a small voice from behind him.

Jury turned to see a lad of perhaps twelve with a tray held around his neck. It was filled with various snacks: peanuts, Twix bars, and so forth. "Not really. Do you?"

"Any o' yours?" The gum in his mouth was apparently not enough. He grabbed another pack from his tray.

"What?"

"Business?"

"Yeah." Jury pulled out his warrant card and thrust it in front of the boy's face.

The mouth dropped open; the stick of gum slid out of its wrapping faster than a gun from a holster. "Bloody hell."

"You must be Joey. The one who sells snacks to the customers inside?"

Joey gave only a half nod, as if fearful a full one might land him in the nick.

"Don't worry, Joey. All I want is a bit of information about how you sell this stuff. You go inside and start at the back?"

Then Joey nodded a good half dozen times. "Right. Straight through them up to the front. I don't make change; if they don't have the right money, I just let them have whatever and collect next time. It's kind of an honor system." Joey seemed proud of that.

"So you could say you just make a kind of beeline from back to front?"

"Bloody hell," Joey said again. "You're talking about that guy who got himself shot the other night. Well, Twick'am police have already been all over me about that as it happened right after I got up to the front. Whew! I was lucky I didn't get it meself."

"You certainly were, Joey. I'm glad you're okay. It must have been harrowing."

"Exciting" was more like it. Look at all the attention. He was on his way to being a star.

Jury smiled. "Nice to talk to you, Joey; I probably will want you again. Are you free to come to the Yard?"

Was Jury kidding?

# PART II
# Roadtrip

# 28

Manchester was about two hundred miles or four hours away from London. Before he left, Wiggins had asked his mum to make sure she was by herself and that others were out of the house when he got there, so he would not have to deal with a barrage of comments and questions about himself, his job, or them. Wiggins gathered up his keys and a bag with clothes in it that looked like a black doctor's bag and left his flat.

He always enjoyed his journeys to Manchester because he was alone. He didn't have his boss sitting beside him scoffing at the neon-bright lights of a Happy Eater. So Wiggins looked forward with high expectations to a cuppa or, better, beans on toast. He could just feel his boss stiffening at the idea of stopping, but on his journey alone, he could stop whenever he liked.

Whenever he liked was whenever he saw a sign for a Happy Eater or a Little Chef. However, what he had to deal with now were unengaging signs attached to unhospitable-looking eateries further attached to enormous petrol stations.

He managed to weep his way through as he was mourning the absence of the Little Chefs and the Happy Eaters, which had been replaced by Starbucks, Greggs, and one or two other unwelcoming rest-stop eateries. However, all he wanted was a cuppa tea, and if he couldn't get it from a Little Chef or a Happy Eater, he would have to settle for one of these debased cups at what he considered the down-market rest stops that he passed one after the other. He got off the motorway at the next petrol station, where he saw a number of take-out places and coffee shops. One of which was Starbucks, which he refused to enter. He would not have gone into Starbucks if he'd been lost in the desert for a week, so he settled on Greggs, where he got himself three cups of tea accompanied by an ambitiously iced pastry, which he didn't really want but which he bought to make the three cups look good. Then he paid his bill and left. He pulled into the petrol station just to make it look like car maintenance was the whole point of stopping at this exit. The gas was hardly needed, since his tank had been filled before he left London, but he liked to convince himself that he did have some business at hand other than drinking tea.

After he paid and left the petrol station, Wiggins drove back to the M6, headed to Northampton. He spent the next hour thinking of his sister Betty Jean, wondering how she could have waited five years to send a postcard to her mum. Five years and no communication with her family. Betty Jean had always been forgetful, though one could hardly call five years an absence of forgetfulness. He had never understood Betty Jean's failure to remember birthdays and holidays, because she was generally a very kind person who would really bend over backwards to help someone.

Wiggins was lost in thoughts about his sister when he realized he was halfway to Manchester. He decided he needed to get some gas, but he knew this was his excuse to get his cuppa. He saw a Welcome Break and took the exit. He was mildly familiar with Welcome Breaks, and though he didn't approve of them, it was certainly better than nothing. He pulled in, got out of his car, and went inside the Welcome Break, picking up one of their paper menus and reading it through. They didn't have much of a tea selection. He couldn't believe the Welcome Break was offering Earl Grey. That was something Starbucks would do, being an American firm that had no idea that not every Englishman was wedded to Earl Grey. He sat down at the counter and ordered his cuppa together with a tasteless bun that bore some resemblance to a jammy but wasn't one. It was enough to take a bite from it and wash it down with tea, which of course had been made with the exact proportions of milk and sugar. He paid his bill and left, then pulled into the petrol station and filled his tank.

He wasn't far from Birmingham. He hated Birmingham. He wondered how many roundabouts he was going to have to negotiate just to get through it. Now, if there had still been a Little Chef at every roundabout, he could have stopped at all of them, but of course that was just a dream. Oh dear. Why did things have to change?

Back on the M6 he promised himself there would be no more stops until he pulled up outside his mum's house. A promise he knew would be broken into a hundred bits when he saw the turnoff for Wolverhampton. That meant somewhere there was another Welcome Break. He spent the rest of his drive with poignant thoughts of BJ, and how much he had missed dancing with her. They'd made quite a team.

When Wiggins drove up in front of his childhood home, which was nothing but a squinty-looking red-brick row house in one of the lesser suburbs of Manchester, he was absolutely exhausted—not from the lack of his cuppa but from wondering how he could deal with Mum, knowing she would be in quite a state. He climbed out of his car, pulled out the black, medical-looking bag, and walked up to the front steps.

At the top of the narrow stone steps stood Wiggins's mum, Mildred, looking as she had always done. Plump and spry in one of her many dresses, all of the same material, much the same pattern. Sprigs and sprouts of flowers against some dark background. Hard by her side was Hermione Hingle, the cat that belonged to her brother, John Hingle. The cat was big, unkempt, and very much attached to Wiggins's house but not to Wiggins. The cat did not like anybody, including Mildred, her feeder. She showed this by shredding the sofa, clawing her way up and down the curtains, and paying no attention to injunctions such as "Come and eat now, Hermione." The cat's idea of eating was to knife her way through a bag of dry food, spread a lot of it around the floor, and eat it bit by bit. She did not give chase. She let the chase come to her. If a mouse ran by, she did not attempt to kill it but just put out her claw and clobbered it, so the mouse walked way, dazed but alive. No one could understand this odd propensity of Hermione the cat. But then, come on! Who ever understands cats anyway? A cat is not born to be understood. Only to be waited on.

"Alfie. Alfie."

"Hello, Mum." He hugged her and held on to her tightly. He wasn't sure which one of them was holding the other one up.

"You'll find out about her, won't you, dear?"

"Sure, Mum. I'm a cop, remember?"

After Mildred rushed to Wiggins to embrace him, Hermione rushed in the manner of a dog, meaning she clutched onto a tree trunk and peed it to perdition. Done with that, Hermione simply walked away.

"Mum, can you get rid of that cat?" Wiggins hoped Hermione hadn't heard him say this. God knows what the results would be. There had been rushed thoughts on Wiggins's part that the cat had appeared at the exact time Betty Jean had disappeared, but that hardly bore thinking about.

"Why would I get rid of that cat? She's company."

"Company? Mum. She doesn't do any of the things company or companion cats usually do. I never hear her purr. I haven't seen her sit on your lap or cuddle up to you."

"Of course not. Does that sound like Hermione, Alfie?"

Wiggins thought this discussion was just going around in circles, so he went to the subject of the postcard.

"Just let me see the card." He sat down in one of the worn, flowered, crouton-colored easy chairs in their small living room as his mother handed him the postcard. It had a picture of Cornwall on the front, and that of course told them absolutely nothing. Sometimes he thought every postcard in England had a picture of Cornwall on the front. He turned it over and read the message.

"Dear Mum, I know how you must feel." Wiggins stopped reading. She knows how her mum must feel? Apparently not. But he didn't say this. "I can only say I am dreadfully sorry, but not to worry. I know I've been gone for a long time, and I do apologize Mum for not getting in touch sooner. Do you still have that trophy on your mantle from the dance contest we won? Oh, those were the days. All my love, Betty Jean."

Wiggins thought he would have gladly throttled Betty Jean. After all this time, just an obscure message that could have come from someone who was taking a week's vacation. He paused and took a deep breath, then said, "She's not really telling us much, is she?"

"No, she isn't."

Wiggins sighed quietly and went to sit beside his mother. "She will be back soon, Mum." He turned the card over again to look at the postmark. He simply could not read it. It looked as if the last two letters were an *l* and an *e*. He sighed. Suddenly, he sat up straight and thought, My God. Macalvie. Exeter. Commander Macalvie. Here was the place to get help. Wiggins knew Macalvie's number by heart.

# 29

"Macalvie," said Brian Macalvie on his end of the line in Exeter.

"Mr. Macalvie," said Wiggins.

"Wiggins?" said Macalvie. "Well, it's good to hear from you. I haven't seen you in, what, weeks?"

"I called to ask a favor of you."

"Go right ahead."

"First, I've got to give you some background information, but that shouldn't take too long. Do you have five minutes?"

"You know I've got time for you, Wiggins. So let's have it. What's the favor?"

"This involves my sister in Manchester."

"I didn't know you had a sister in Manchester."

"Part of the difficulty here is that at the moment she's not in Manchester."

"Well, where the hell is she?" There was a pause and a sound of *glug, glug, glug,* then a small belch, and Macalvie took a guess. "Are you drinking Bromo Seltzer?"

"Yes. Sorry, Commander. I've got a hell of a headache."

"Yeah. You're passing it all along to me. Now, go on about your sister."

"The thing is, she has disappeared."

"What?" Surprised, he accidentally shoved a stack of folders from his desk. "Disappeared? When did this happen? Yesterday? Last week?"

Wiggins gave an embarrassed little laugh. "She disappeared five years ago."

"Five years? And you are just getting around to calling me now?"

"Well, the thing is, nothing really happened until now."

"You're saying your sister disappeared five years ago; let's go back there."

"Yes. That would be a good idea. Five years ago, on Christmas Day, we were downstairs. We were unwrapping presents and BJ—that's my sister's name, Betty Jean—suddenly said she felt ill. She ran upstairs to her bedroom. As I told you, this was Christmas Day. You can imagine how many doctors wanted to come out on the holiday, but we finally got one who came out, looked at BJ, and diagnosed her with a stomach bug. Some sort of stomach upset. He gave her a prescription and said that should take care of it, and if my sister didn't feel better in a couple of days, be sure and call him, or come and see him."

"And?" prompted Macalvie.

"That's just the thing, sir. When we went up to her room the next day to check on her, she wasn't there. She had disappeared."

"Oh, come on, Wiggins. 'Disappear' is a very big word. What do you mean she disappeared? She climbed out the window? She let herself down the side of the building with a rope. What the hell happened?"

"I don't know. I just don't know."

"Well, I assume you looked into her disappearance."

"Of course. We got forensics. We got everything that I could think of."

"And you're telling me it's been five years? And you haven't turned up anything?"

"Until now. Our mum got a card."

"And you're just getting around to calling me? What does your boss say?"

"You mean Superintendent Jury?"

"Well, last I heard, he was your boss. Yes, Jury. What does Jury say?"

"The thing is, when it happened, I told him she died."

"Wiggins. This just gets more and more curious. Why did you tell him that?"

"I guess I didn't want to tell him she disappeared."

"Are you saying that right now he doesn't know any of this? He doesn't know what you've just told me?"

"I'm afraid that's right, sir."

"Hold on a minute, Wiggins. I think I heard a knock." Macalvie put the receiver against his shoulder. The thought of a knock was about all it was, like a knock begrudged. "Yeah," said Macalvie to the knock. Gilly Thwaite opened the door and stuck her head around the edge.

"No, Gilly," said Macalvie.

"Oh, come on, Guv. You don't even know what I want."

"Of course I know. It's about fingerprints. I told you before it's a public call box."

"I know it is," said Gilly, "and she used it at exactly six oh seven."

"You don't know that."

"Yes, I do," said Gilly.

"Okay, Gilly. Come back after you've eliminated the five hundred and ninety-nine other prints on that call box." Her head disappeared, and she closed the door. "Well, for once," said Macalvie to the receiver, "she gave up pretty easily."

"What's that, Gilly Thwaite?" said Wiggins. "She never gives up."

"Well, sometimes she pretends to, then comes back later with another absurd argument, but anyway, go on about your sister. Back to square one. She disappeared from her room that night—at least, it was probably that night. You didn't check on her until the next day?"

"Yes."

"Can you think of any significant event which has happened between the last time you saw her and now?"

There was a long pause, which Macalvie broke by saying, "Look, you say you didn't see her. She didn't come downstairs or walk out the door, but surely there's one more entrance to your house."

"Well, there was a back door that led to a small garden and a walk, and the walk led around to the road in front."

"Well, there you are, Wiggins. That's what happened. She went through the back door and out to the road."

"Oh, I don't think so, sir. I don't think BJ would have done that without saying something to Mum."

"But that's why you said she 'disappeared' in the first place. Can't you assume that it's possible your sister pretended to be sick because that's what she wanted everyone to think, and when the doctor left, she got up, went down to the kitchen and out the door, possibly to meet someone?"

"But whom?" said Wiggins.

"Wiggins, for heaven's sake, she is *your* sister. I wouldn't know. She had a man or a boyfriend, did she?"

"Not that I know of."

"I don't think you know very much in the first place. If you say your sister has disappeared, then whom did she know—whom might she have gone to this much trouble for? Because this is the sort of thing you do if you have a guy your family does not approve of."

"My God. She was hardly fifteen."

"'Hardly fifteen' means she was fifteen."

"Well, that's a little young, isn't it?"

"Oh, come on, Wiggins! She could've taken the rattle out of her mouth to kiss someone."

"Ho ho, very funny."

"Well, the point is, she needed a reason for pretending to be sick, and the reason could have been to get out of her room to meet someone."

"But we're not in those times."

"No, we're here in these times. And a fifteen-year-old girl could've fallen in love with an older man or a boy her age."

"I don't think so, Mr. Macalvie—"

"You're not thinking at all, Wiggins. I haven't heard anything from you that demonstrates you've really given any thought to this disappearance. I mean, for God's sake, you know her. I don't."

"That's true, Mr. Macalvie. I forgot to mention she loved dancing. She was a grand dancer, BJ was. We both were. We used to dance together all the time. Indeed, we won several dancing contests. But the thing is, Mr. Macalvie, let's say she did go with someone on a trip; she wouldn't have stayed silent about it for five years!"

"No. I agree. She wouldn't. First of all, you have to find out what initially happened before you can speculate about what's happening five or six years later. So that's what to work on. Now, you said the two of you liked to dance?"

"Yes. We did."

"And where is the last place you did some serious dancing?"

"Well, I guess maybe at Honey's Dance Hall."

"Where in the hell is that?"

"In Lyme Regis."

"Now, what about this postcard?"

"BJ sent it to my mum, or rather *our* mum, in Manchester."

"Manchester? What are you doing in Manchester?"

"That's where we live. It's where my mum lives."

"Manchester? People don't really live in Manchester, Wiggins. I mean, there are people there. They hold down jobs. I guess they are getting married. They have kids and houses, but I mean, they don't really live there."

"Oh, come on, Mr. Macalvie. What about Manchester United?"

"What about it? You don't call that living, do you?"

"You know something, Mr. Macalvie? Did anyone ever tell you you were a snob?"

"Yes, but no one has ever told me twice. So come on. It's going to take you about three or four hours to get from Manchester, where nobody lives, to Exeter."

"Yes," said Wiggins. "Where people really live."

"It's after four o'clock so why don't you spend the night at your mother's. Get some sleep so you can leave Manchester around four a.m. and arrive at my office in Exeter by eight a.m. We should get to Mousehole by ten a.m."

"Okay," said Wiggins.

"I'll see you tomorrow, and bring the damn card with you." Macalvie slammed down the receiver.

# 30

Jury thought the Old Wine Shades pub would be relatively empty at this early hour, and he was right. For once he found a place to park on the street in front.

There were only a dozen or so people at the bar. Harry Johnson wasn't on his usual bar stool—which must have had a RESERVED sign hanging over it, for Jury had never seen anyone else sitting there.

The Old Wine Shades was unusually quiet this evening, not from a lack of conversation, but because the conversation was at such a low key. As if everybody were trying not to divulge secrets.

"It's like a den of spies, Trevor," said Jury to the Shades' wine expert. He didn't belong to the bar, but that's where he worked.

Trevor was polishing the wine bottles, as he usually did, to light-reflecting splendor. "Superintendent! Good to see you. What can I get you?"

"Oh, just a pint of something. Your expression says that 'a pint' would only be of 'something.'"

"Come on, Mr. Jury, I'm not that bad, am I? Some beers are very good."

"Hm. 'Good,' but not 'worthy,' is my guess."

"There's a really good stout, Speedway, that'll only set you back about twenty quid."

"A *pint*?" At Trevor's nod, Jury said, "Might as well buy the whole brewery. Who makes it?"

"Craft brewery in San Diego. Bit for bit, it's pricier than this." Trevor parked a bottle of vodka on the bar.

"Good lord! Can I afford it?"

Trevor laughed. "I can give you a half or even a third of a pint. See if you like it."

"I hope I don't. A cop's pay stretches about as far as Adman's."

"You're more than a cop."

"Not enough more that I can drink that beer."

But Trevor had already set a half-pint under the beer pulls and was pulling down on the tap. "If you don't think it's worth it, you don't pay. How's that?"

"Fine, except I'm sure I'll think it's worth it."

"You can always lie." Trevor slid the glass over in front of him.

Jury took a drink. "My lord, Trevor. That's wonderful."

"I told you to lie. But let me see now . . . discounted . . ." Trevor pretended to turn this over.

"Since when do you discount?"

"To New Scotland Yard? Always. You never knew it because Mr. Johnson pays for the wine. He's so obsessed with it. That half-pint will cost you three quid."

"That's not half of twenty."

"It's the discount. Come on, three quid." Trevor held out his hand.

Jury slapped a fiver into it. "Please keep the change. Five is cheap just for finding out there's this incredible beer—what's it called?"

"Speedway. Made in California. We import it over here. There are some others, even pricier—"

"A hundred and fifty quid a bottle. I'd say so."

But Trevor was shaking his head. "That's not what I meant. Not rich in price, but in meaning. Except this is rum. Means the same thing, more or less."

Jury's eyes widened. "My God, Trevor. I think you've hit it!"

Jury drew out a money clip, tossed a couple of notes on the bar.

"Well, I'm glad to be of help, Superintendent, but that's an ocean too much money for a pint of Adman's. Or anything."

"Nothing's too much. I'll tell you later. I've got to go." Jury was halfway to the door.

"Shall I tell Mr. Johnson—"

But Jury didn't hear or care about telling Mr. J. He was in his car and calling Boring's.

# 31

"*Boeuf Richelieu Madeira?* What in hell's that?"

"I don't know," said Melrose. "It's a very classy French thing Boring's chef thought we'd like."

"First time I've noticed anything new."

"For God's sakes, don't be so disgruntled. It can't always be *blanquette de veau* or Dover sole."

"Why not?" said Jury. "Boring's is not an innovative restaurant. It's been here for decades, serving the same tea, the same drinks, the same food."

"What about the Portobello mushroom you found such an alien dish?"

"So did you. Boring's should stick to the regular stuff."

"I'll tell the chef 'the regular stuff.' He'll appreciate that. Or maybe I could ask Santos for a few regular recipes."

"Oh, be quiet. And speaking of food, I haven't told you about my interview with Brad Ross."

"So tell me. What does it have to do with food?"

Jury gave him the details of his talk with Ross.

Melrose looked astonished. "My God, you really *are* a detective!"

"You'd never have guessed." Jury plucked a small slice of French bread from the bread tray and spread a knifeful of butter on it.

"Well, I'd surely never have timed a man's movements by a soufflé's settling."

"I wouldn't either, were the Rosses not so devoted to their cook. She's been around as long as Boring's." Jury held the buttered bread in front of his mouth without eating it.

"Ross could have done all this in twenty minutes?"

"Yes. I timed it. Seven minutes there, the same back. That leaves six."

"But the actual shooting—six minutes might be plenty of time for an expert shooter like you—"

"Me? I'm terrible. I couldn't hit that post right over there." He nodded toward a mahogany post not ten feet away, in front of which sat a table for two that, when occupied, was always occupied by Colonel Neame and Major Champs, who sat there now. Jury nodded to them and then looked up at Young Higgins, who had come to their table looking quite pleased, at least for Young Higgins.

"I'm happy to announce we've a new dish this evening that is quite wonderful. A beef Richelieu in Madeira sauce." Higgins then went into detail about its preparation and ingredients.

As if deep in thought, Jury said, "That's a bit rich."

"Indeed, sir, it is. Not to everyone's taste."

"I didn't mean . . ." said Jury, his mind starting to click as if it were snapping photos. Click: Trevor's cocktail. He pulled out his mobile and, ignoring Melrose's warning that mobile calls weren't allowed in the dining room, tapped in a number.

"Trevor? This is Richard Jury. I know I just left the Shades, but I've something to ask you about that cocktail I didn't drink: The Bacardi—was that a *white* rum? . . . So, do you use that in many drinks? . . . Cocktails, mostly. Did you ever hear of an Aruba-Cuba? Stupid name, I agree, but—" Jury nodded and made sounds of concurrence, then said, "Okay, thanks, Trevor. You've no idea what a help you've been."

"I've no idea either," said Melrose when Jury hung up. "What were you talking about?"

"When we saw Major Champs in Boring's, maybe what he said wasn't 'That's a bit rich.' Maybe he said, 'That's a bit rum.' That's what I was trying to remember."

"What was that about white rum? I didn't know there was a white rum."

"When you think of rum, what color do you picture? I always think of something the color of molasses, or at least amber. Not white. That's why it didn't occur to me, why my mind blanked it out."

"Blanked what out?"

"The bottle on the bar, or the bottle Lloyd was just taking off the bar. At the Red Queen."

"The point being . . . ?"

"The point being that we've been baffled as to why the killer would have chosen to shoot Tom Treadnor in such a difficult way, when he could easily have shot him at home or out in the barn or getting out of his car. But he couldn't."

"No? Why?"

"Because it wasn't him."

# 32

"*What?* You're saying it wasn't Tom Treadnor? But . . . she identified him!" Melrose exclaimed.

"I know. The victim looked like him. Listen—"

But Melrose didn't. He said, "You're not going to tell me Treadnor had a twin brother!"

"No, I'm not going to tell you that. But there is, or was, a man who worked in the city who looked exactly like him, except for the hair color and the eyes. They were often mistaken for each other. There's a pub in Docklands where once a week they invite different musicians, sometimes one, sometimes two—you know, like a sax player, a drummer, a trombonist, a piano player—to play. This pub is popular with the young crowd, a lot of whom live in those pricey high-rises around Bridge and

London Station. Treadnor mentioned it to his wife. Said he walked in and saw a guy playing piano who looked just like him. So it wasn't just the looks. Treadnor used to play piano in a trio. I mean, wouldn't that give you pause?"

"As to what?"

"Wouldn't you think you were seeing a mirror image of yourself?"

"I don't play the piano."

"Very funny."

"So what's this cocktail business you were talking about?"

"When he was shot, the murder victim was drinking something called an Aruban Cuban, according to the barman. The bottle was sitting on the bar. Only Treadnor hated rum. He drank everything else, but not rum."

"So this fellow at the bar was the other guy, the one Treadnor had seen in Docklands? But what kind of a coincidence is *that*?"

"I didn't say it was a coincidence."

"The guy was *supposed* to be there?"

"I think so."

"Sitting in Tom's seat?"

Jury nodded. "And everybody thought he was Treadnor."

Melrose frowned. "But there are all sorts of ways of identifying a body."

"Of course there are. But why would anyone want to? After his wife identified him?"

Melrose's frown deepened. "Are you saying it was a *plot*?"

"Sure."

"You think she did it for the inheritance?"

When Jury nodded, Melrose said, "But if she'd been convicted, she wouldn't have inherited a penny."

"Of course not."

"And what about what's-his-name? Jason . . . ?"

"Lederer. He was sent to Chicago by his firm to open a new branch of the agency."

"And did he get there?"

"Oh, he got there all right. But just turned around and took some holiday time to go somewhere—Cancún, I think it was. He didn't give the office any exact information."

"And you think he just came back to the U.K. and wound up in the Red Queen?"

"Definitely. That was the plan. If anyone tried to follow up on his 'holiday' plan, they'd have come up against a stone wall."

"But at some point, he'd have had to turn up and answer questions."

"About what? Not about the Treadnor case. What had he to do with that?"

"I just don't get it."

"The Treadnor inheritance. The twenty-million-pound trust his father left that he couldn't get his hands on. Unless he died, that is. In the event of his death, Alice gets it."

"But we were just saying—not if she killed him."

"She didn't. She killed Jason Lederer."

# 33

When Wiggins finally walked into Brian Macalvie's office in Exeter, Macalvie was sitting in a heap in a swivel chair with his feet planted up on his desk. "Okay, Wiggins. You drove for hours to show me something, so let us see it."

Wiggins handed over the card that his mother had received the previous morning from Betty Jean. "This card was from my sister, Betty Jean. As I have told you, she hasn't appeared for five years. We'd had no word from her until my mother got this card, and I thought there might be some clues that I can't pick up but that your forensics people could."

Macalvie took the card. "Mmm. I can't make out the name of the place because it's so banged up." He was looking at the postal code. Then he looked at the front. "Oh. Cornwall. Well, that shouldn't be a problem. Except," he said, "she is probably not really in Cornwall and just sent this to make your mother feel a little better, though it would seem to me that this would make a person feel worse. So, what do you make of this, Wiggins?"

"What I make of it is that she is trying to both communicate and not communicate. You know, she is telling our mum where it's from, but at the same time, she says not to worry; she's just taking a little trip down memory lane. Now, that would certainly be a clue, wouldn't it?"

"Yeah. Of course, it would. What do you think she means?"

"I've been trying to remember, and I haven't been successful—something we did in Cornwall, or some reason we went to Cornwall many years ago. Wait a minute. Wait a minute," said Wiggins. "Of course, we were in Cornwall because we had entered a dance contest, and it was being held in Mousehole. Do you know how to get to the A30 from here?"

Macalvie said with disgust, "Wiggins, I could get to the moon from here. Of course I know how to get to the A30. So come on. Let's go."

They turned onto the A30 toward Mousehole. After they'd been driving twenty or thirty miles, Macalvie started complaining about the lack of restaurant stops, and Wiggins chimed in with a full monologue on the loss of Little Chefs and Happy Eaters. They had a brief argument over the relative merits of those restaurant chains. Macalvie had preferred the Little Chefs, because the Happy Eaters had both too many bright colors and too many kids in them in sections that were designated for kids. It was only about a two-hour drive to Mousehole, and Macalvie asked again what Wiggins's sister would be doing there. Wiggins told him that it must be part of the memory-lane trip. Macalvie said he couldn't really imagine having memories you would want to relive from a trip to Mousehole.

"Well," said Wiggins, "I think I told you she was a great dancer. I was too."

"Now, that I can't imagine. You mean the two of you danced together. Your sister, Betty Jean, sounds like a right treat, Wiggins. She leaves the house without a word, and nobody has seen her for five years, so finally she sends her mum a postcard from Mousehole. Still doesn't tell her anything. I mean, for God's sake."

"How long," said Wiggins, "since you've seen your mother?"

"Me? I don't have one."

"Why doesn't that surprise me? You know, I'm wondering if this whole memory-lane thing could be BJ's way of going to the places we went together and danced, and one of them was in Mousehole."

"Mowsel," said Macalvie. Wiggins paid no attention to this correction and just went on. "The contest there was huge, with a lot of contenders. Did I tell you we won?"

"I guess you're telling me now."

"The first-place prize statuette is still sitting on Mum's mantle." They drove on as Wiggins described this dance contest.

When they got to the outskirts of Mousehole, Macalvie slowed the car to ask directions from an old man with two canes who looked like someone who didn't want to give them, but then finally spoke up: "You mean the Mowsel post office?"

Macalvie said to the old man, "That's right. Can you tell us where it is?"

"I can tell you. You go down to Northcliff."

"Okay. Do you live here?" said Macalvie.

"In Mowsel?" said the old man. Where else would "here" be, wondered Wiggins.

"Yes."

"Lived here all my life. Man and boy, ninety years." The old man looked like he might have sprouted wings. "Greatest little place in England." Wiggins wondered if he knew other places in England.

"Yes," said Macalvie. "I've always liked this place."

Wiggins wondered why; it was craggy, hilly, and full of sea air. What was there to like? He supposed it was quaintness. Mousehole was one of the quaintest small towns he had ever visited.

Tourists must eat it up.

# 34

Macalvie pulled up outside the Mousehole post office. There were no other people except for a woman who Wiggins assumed was the postmistress, as she was sorting through mails, pushing envelopes here and there on a long deal table.

Macalvie took out his identification card and showed it to her. "I beg your pardon, madam, but is there anyone here today who would have been working here five years ago?"

She looked at his ID, then at him, and laughed. "I couldn't tell you anyone who was here five days ago."

"I take it you are saying it's not a popular job."

"Ha," she said. "There's no music playing. There's nothing here except mail."

"Well, maybe you can help us, Miss . . . ?"

"Coy. Hilda Coy. I doubt it."

"Just give it a try, Ms. Coy." Macalvie showed her the picture of Wiggins's sister. "Do you think you've ever seen this woman?"

She adjusted her little glasses over her piglike eyes and said, "You know, she looks familiar. Let me think."

"By all means," said Macalvie.

"Wait a minute," called the postmistress across the room. "Yes, I remember. Bunny-Jean?"

Wiggins corrected her. "No. It's Betty Jean."

"Yes. Betty Jean. She worked here for nearly a year. She was my assistant."

"She isn't here anymore."

"No."

"Do you know where she went?"

"No, but maybe Brenda knows."

"Who is Brenda?" said Macalvie.

"Brenda Barnstorm. She's the assistant postmistress now. Well, I can't really call her that. She's only been working here for a few months. She took Betty Jean's place. Brenda is really good. She's got some sort of extra sense."

"Meaning?" asked Macalvie.

"Brenda can hold a letter up to the light as if she can see right through it. She can tell a lot about the sender by the name and address written on the outside. She can look at the letters and the way they were written, and the ink. She's good on ink.

She can tell the difference between the kinds of ink, and what they must mean. Honestly, she can read people like a book. She should be along here anytime now."

"Did Brenda know Betty Jean well?" said Wiggins.

"No, I don't think she knew her at all, to tell the truth. She came and Betty Jean left. Here she comes now."

A young woman was coming through the door. She was thin, with a fishy-looking face and small eyes. She wore big glasses and had an adenoidal voice.

"Brenda," said Hilda Coy. "These gentlemen were looking for Betty Jean Wiggins. You know, the one that you replaced."

"Oh yes, Betty Jean." She did not embellish upon the name. She just went over to the table where Hilda had been working and started sorting.

"You talked to her, didn't you?"

"You mean Betty Jean?"

"Yes. You took her place; you must have had some kind of conversation with her," said Macalvie.

"No. I never had any conversations with her. I don't really know anything about her."

"That surprises me," said Macalvie. "According to Ms. Coy, you could read people like a book, and you could read mail without opening envelopes."

Brenda just shrugged and sorted the mail.

"You have no idea where Betty Jean might have gone?" asked Wiggins.

"No. Now, if you look at this envelope," she said, holding an envelope in such a way that no one else could look at it except her. "Whoever wrote this letter to Evelyn Sheperd—the name on the envelope—is an extremely well-organized, dependable, and rational person. Look at the way the *i*'s are dotted, and the *t*'s are crossed. They are all written exactly in the right place."

Macalvie looked. "Yes, that's where people usually put the *i*'s and cross the *t*'s. Even I do it."

"But the point is, whoever was writing this letter to Evelyn does it so consistently."

"Oh," said Macalvie, "you mean every time there is an *i*, she dotted it, and every time there is a *t*, she crossed it? But do you know who wrote the letter?"

"No. I can't read the return address."

"But I get the impression you don't have to be able to read the return addresses. You just know. I mean, look at the way you're analyzing the *i*'s and *t*'s. It's really quite amazing. I should have you on my SOCO team."

"What's SOCO?" asked Brenda Barnstorm.

"SOCO. It's the Scene of Crimes Outfit. They try to gather evidence from the scenes of crimes."

"Oh, I could probably do that, but I couldn't really leave my position here. I am too necessary for Ms. Coy." Here Brenda looked at Hilda Coy, waiting for confirmation of this. Hilda nodded her head in a way that suggested "probably."

Wiggins was looking at her head, and he couldn't tell whether it was making a shake or a nod. It was someplace in between. Macalvie rooted through the letters on the mail table, picked out one that was addressed to a William Smithson, and handed it to Brenda. "Okay, what about this one? Why have you got your eyes shut?"

"I'm listening to my voices. There are a number of them, and they tell me about different ways of writing. And of course the ink is important. This ink on this one tells me the writer is a little careless."

"Where do you get that?" said Wiggins.

"Look at the envelope. A couple of smears. The *m*'s and the *s*'s on 'Smithson.'"

Macalvie said, "Look, what is your evidence for the conclusion you come to about the writers?"

"Evidence?" said Brenda. "I've just been telling you, haven't I? Look at the *t*'s and the *i*'s."

Now Wiggins reached into his pocket and brought out the card. He started handing it to Brenda, saying, "Here is something written by my sister. The person we are trying to find."

Macalvie pushed Wiggins's hands back. "Just a moment, Sergeant. Are we sure Ms. Barnstorm is ready for something as difficult as this?"

"Oh," said Brenda, "for me there's no difficulty, especially when my voices are helping."

Macalvie cleared his throat and said, "The thing is, Ms. Barnstorm, I would like to hear the evidence for your conclusions. If you think you can manage that, we will produce the postcard."

"Thank you very much, Mr. . . . What is your name?"

"Macalvie. Actually, Divisional Commander of the Devon and Cornwall Constabulary."

"Well, that certainly sounds important."

"It is," said Macalvie. "Now, go ahead and look at this postcard." Wiggins completed his handover of BJ's postcard. Brenda Barnstorm took it. Held it up to the light and read it. Turned it this way and that. Remarked on the picture of Cornwall on the front, and how she wasn't sure that this was a good representation of Mousehole.

"Carry on," said Macalvie.

Brenda cleared her throat and said, "After reading the message, well, I can certainly say with conviction—here is the evidence—the writer of this letter really loves her mum. You can tell she is a devoted daughter—"

Macalvie interrupted. "How can you tell that?"

"Because she says that she is very sorry she hasn't been in touch before and she hopes her mum will forgive her for not writing for so long. Now, if you look at the way she forms her *l*'s, you will see she is upright, no-nonsense, and perfectly in command of the alphabet. And of course, her *i*'s are liberally dotted—not just one little pinch like a grain of pepper over the *i*, but a fulsome, showy dot."

"What about the *t*'s?" said Macalvie.

"The *t*'s are clean and well-kept and honest."

"Honest?" said Macalvie. "It's a long time since I've seen a *t* I would describe as honest."

"You've certainly got one here, Mr. Macalvie." Brenda turned the card and put it close to Macalvie's face.

"You see? You see that *t*?" Macalvie refused to answer.

"So, we have a young woman. What was her name?"

"I call her BJ. Her name is Betty Jean Wiggins."

"All right, here is a young woman who is fond of her mother. Believes very much in keeping in touch with people." In the background, Macalvie snorted.

"Now," said Macalvie, "can you tell us where she might be?"

"Hmm," said Brenda. "She might be in Penzance."

"Why do you say that?"

"Well, Penzance is pretty close. If she's going anywhere along the coast, she is likely to go to Penzance."

Macalvie couldn't stand it any longer and he took out one of his cigars. When Hilda Coy said, "Oh excuse me, sir, but we don't think smoking is appropriate in the post office," Macalvie simply continued to roll his cigar. Put it into his mouth. Got out his lighter and said before he lit it, "You might not, Ms. Coy, your psychic clairvoyant and her voices might not, but I do." Macalvie lit the cigar and started puffing away.

"Well," said Ms. Coy, "I think I must ask you to leave the post office if you insist on doing that."

"Yes, that's all right," said Macalvie. "But I wonder if you just happen to think anything at all that would further our finding Betty Jean Wiggins."

"While she was working here, I believe she lived at Tasker's guesthouse. You might go along there and ask Isabel Tasker."

"Where is Tasker's?"

"It is just around the corner and up the street. It's a guesthouse. Sort of a bed-and-breakfast."

"Thank you very much," said Wiggins. "We will probably go and check this guesthouse."

As Wiggins and Macalvie were leaving the post office, Macalvie suddenly whipped around and said, "Good God, we didn't get the information from Brenda Barnstorm, and I imagine she'd be the one to ask."

"About what?" said Wiggins.

"About the strange moaning sound we heard apparently from the woman who was standing on the pavement. Remember?"

"Yes. How could I forget."

Macalvie turned around and described to Brenda the woman they saw, who was standing in the street, letting out an incredible howling sound. Macalvie then said, "I couldn't figure out if it was a couple of cats in a fight or Sergeant Wiggins having an allergy attack or a coyote."

Brenda Barnstorm turned to him and said, "A coyote? How could a coyote ever get to Mousehole?"

"You did. Didn't you?"

She turned away. Macalvie said, "All right. All right. You think you know what it was?"

"Of course. So would you if you lived in Mousehole. It was old Mrs. Everts, who once in a while gets the inclination to stop wherever she is, when she's out walking, to let out this little howl. It's the sound of the Mousehole cat. You never heard of the Mousehole cat?"

"No, Brenda. I never did," said Macalvie.

Brenda immediately plunged into the story of the Mousehole cat, who lived with old Tom. The cat would make melodic sounds that could be heard across the waves and amid high winds. It was believed that these sounds could lead sailors and fishermen to safety during storms.

"I'd sooner believe in the coyote," said Macalvie. "Okay, Wiggins. Let's go."

The woman who opened the door of Tasker's was small, dark, dumpy, and unhappy-looking. "Yes," she said.

Wiggins decided against taking out his ID and saw Macalvie had not taken his out either. Police presence could be a real put-off. The petite, dark-haired woman invited them in and asked them if they were looking for accommodations. Wiggins said, "No, we aren't. We're looking for a former guest of yours."

"Who is that?" said Mrs. Tasker (if this was Mrs. Tasker).

"A young woman named Betty Jean Wiggins. She is my sister."

"Really? And you say she stayed here?"

"Yes. She was here for some time."

"Betty Jean, Betty Jean." Mrs. Isabel Tasker dropped her head in her hands.

Macalvie noticed that on the coffee table in front of the sofa sat, among other things, a crystal ball on a piece of dark-blue velvet. Oh my God, don't let her reach for that! She didn't. She looked up at Wiggins, her face a little brighter, and said, "I'm trying to remember where Betty Jean went."

"That's what we'd like to know," said Wiggins. "Where did she go?"

"Just a minute. Just a minute." She dropped her head in her hands again. "Are you sure her name was Betty Jean?"

"Yes. We were told that she had stayed here at Tasker's for nearly a year, or even more."

"Oh, maybe it was the person who had this job before."

Macalvie thought, Hell! We are not going to deal with job replacements, retirements, and quitting. He said to the Tasker woman, "Did you see her leaving?"

Mrs. Tasker said, "Yes. I remember. I remember it was a rainy, dark afternoon, and she had her bags packed in the car, but then I don't remember—"

Then Macalvie said, "Don't think about it, just try and picture it, the way she looked and then, when she left, if she got into the car. Try and picture that."

Mrs. Tasker said, "Oh, yes. She was getting into her car, and I asked her where she was going. Lyme Regis."

"Lyme Regis?" said Wiggins. "Did she say why she was going to Lyme Regis?"

"Well. Let me think."

Oh, don't think, thought Macalvie. But she dropped her head in her hands and thought and thought. Then she said, "I believe Betty Jean said something about a man or someone she was going to meet there."

"Did she mention any names?"

"No. She didn't say anything about him. It was just somebody she was going to meet."

"Okay," said Macalvie. "Thank you very much. Come on, Wiggins. Let's go."

"How far is Lyme Regis from here?" said Wiggins.

"Three hours. You can get on the A30 and take it to the motorway."

Wiggins and Macalvie thanked Isabel Tasker as they left.

# 35

Before they got to Lyme Regis, Wiggins announced that he was feeling a little peckish. All the talk about Little Chef and Happy Eater had only increased his peckishness and his irritation that they were no longer in existence. He drove on for another four or five miles, came to a roundabout, and saw that at the end of one of the exits was a Hog & Hedge. "Oh, have you tried that, Mr. Macalvie?"

"Tried what?"

"The Hog & Hedge. They are extremely popular. Their food is exceptional, especially the breakfasts. Would it be okay if we stop?"

"Hell, yes. Stop. I'm hungry too and we could be working late into the evening. I could eat a hog."

They exited the roundabout, drove a short distance to the entrance of the huge petrol station, filled up the tank, then parked the car and went inside the Hog & Hedge. It was certainly not hurting for customers. Given so many of the inferior little cafés that had been thrown up beside service stations, Wiggins could understand the popularity of this restaurant, which catered not only to those who favored rations of bacon, chorizo, and chops, but also to vegetarians.

The customers appeared to be happy beyond measure, which is unusual in one of these roadside cafés, where the quality of the food is mediocre and the service is less than friendly, and where the objective seems to be to get people out almost as soon as they sit. But in the Hog & Hedge, this was not the experience at all. Indeed, Macalvie said, he wished to God these servers and counter people would stop smiling. He felt as if he had been dropped into Happyville.

"I don't know, Mr. Macalvie. I thought it was rather pleasant. It's nice to be waited on by people who seem to be waiting on you."

"Seem to. Yes. But of course, they cannot. The smiles are forced. The laughter is forced. The ambience is forced."

Forced it might have been, but that made no odds to either one of them, because they ordered enough food from the Hog & Hedge's overly generous menu to last them through the rest of their trip. Macalvie ordered lamb chops and a mushroom as big as a top hat. A baked potato so full of itself, it looked like it might take off with Macalvie for Honey's Dance Hall and do a few turns.

Wiggins ordered nearly the same thing, but he was stunned by the size of the baked potato, so he got beans on toast instead. Macalvie scoffed. They finished and agreed the food was as good as advertised. They left and continued on their way to Lyme Regis.

The openness and elegance of Lyme Regis did not lessen the charm or the quaintness of craggy little Mousehole. The two places inhabited their own charming universe. The shiny embankment of Lyme Regis, the marine parade, and the crushed-pearl beaches did nothing to undermine the exceptional beauty of Mousehole, except that Lyme Regis possessed the advantage of the spirit of Jane Austen that had been enveloping this town for two centuries. Commerce, of course, had increased in Lyme Regis, so that people might have passed a little boutique called Persuasion without connecting it to Jane Austen's novel.

"No wonder Jane Austen loved this place. Just look at it," said Macalvie. "Yielded. Transparent. Evidently approachable. Don't you agree, Wiggins?"

"Well, I guess so. Up to a point."

When Macalvie said, "What point?" Wiggins wished he hadn't made that comment.

They had both been here before. Macalvie for a murder case, Wiggins for his music. When they got to Lyme Regis, Wiggins was suddenly overcome by memories of the many hours he had spent dancing here with BJ, and the contest they had won at Honey's Dance Hall. They stopped the car in front of a little café. Wiggins got out of the car, went inside, and inquired about Honey's.

"Oh, yes," said the news agent. He got out a local map and drew an arrow. "This is Honey's Dance Hall. It's at the top of the town. It's still open, and people still dance there."

Wiggins thanked him profusely and got back in the car. They drove along the route that the agent had penciled in for them.

Honey's Dance Hall hadn't changed by a hair. It was a long, narrow building that really looked as if it had been made for dancing. Macalvie and Wiggins climbed the wooden steps to the front door, behind which a band was in full swing. They went in.

The halls were studded with framed photographs of dancers looking hilariously happy. Wiggins thought he recognized a few of the faces from the times he and BJ had been here. There were also framed movie posters, one of them featuring Betty Grable and Don Ameche in *Down Argentine Way*. For some reason, this was one of Wiggins's favorites. The small band played tunes from the days of the Second World War. He thought some of them weren't danceable, such as "It's a Long Way to Tipperary," but people danced nevertheless. That's one of the things that interested Wiggins about dancing. Once you started, you just kept on going, not caring especially the direction you were going in. He stopped watching the dancers and started watching the stairs, the long mahogany case to his left, down which came the owner of the dance hall, Honey herself.

If this was Honey, she looked ten years older but not the worse for it. Her graying hair was highlighted with streaks of blond. Her eye makeup was a little overdone, but the rest of her—plumped breasts, thighs, legs—was well composed. She was fighting middle age and, Wiggins thought, winning.

She looked at Wiggins and said, astonished, "Al!" She continued down the stairs and rushed over to where they were standing.

He said, "Hello, Honey. Remember me?"

"How could I possibly forget? You and BJ and that contest. Who's your handsome friend?" At this, Wiggins and Macalvie both looked behind themselves. "Oh, come on," she said. She held out her hand to Macalvie. "Hello, Sweetie. I'm Honey."

Wiggins was stunned that Macalvie could actually answer, "You certainly are. Would you care to dance?" He held out his arms.

"You mean right here? Right now?" The band had started up its CD version of an old Glenn Miller song, "String of Pearls."

"Well, if you are Honey, and this is your dance hall, I would certainly agree. Right here. Right now." Macalvie pushed her to the entrance of the dance hall and twirled her around. There they went. Wiggins, still standing at the entrance to the room, couldn't believe it. Divisional Commander Macalvie, who never took off his coat, dancing.

Macalvie twirled her off, twirled her back, and Wiggins stood there for another ten minutes watching this, until he saw someone cut in and sweep Honey away. Macalvie merely walked back through the dancers to where Wiggins was standing.

"My God, Commander—"

Macalvie stepped into whatever it was Wiggins was going to say. "I do have a life, Wiggins. Indeed, I probably do have a dozen lives you're unacquainted with. Honey remembers you and your sister very well. I got very little information out of her, but I did find out when BJ left here, or at least where she said she was going. She said she was going to Brighton."

Just then, Honey managed to groove her way back to where Wiggins and Macalvie were.

"On her own?" Wiggins said to Honey.

She shrugged. "Far as I know. Come on, let's have a drink."

Macalvie looked down the length of the bar and then brought his eyes back to Honey.

"I was wondering about your hostesses," said Macalvie.

"I just don't care for the sound of 'hostess.' You know its implications."

Macalvie smiled a little. "No, neither do I."

"So what I hire," said Honey, "is dancing partners. That's what they're supposed to be called: dancing partners."

Macalvie looked down the bar again and said, "Those two don't look like they are dancing."

Honey turned and looked. "No. The girls are not supposed to sit at the bar. I thought I'd made that clear, or rather, I tried to make that clear when I talked to them about what they are supposed to do."

"That one apparently didn't hear you." The girl was laughing and picking up a glass. Macalvie assumed it wasn't just Coke.

Honey said, "I don't hire anyone under the age of eighteen."

Macalvie thought the one sitting at the bar didn't look old enough to be feeding herself, much less drinking with a man three times her age.

"You just ask them their age and you buy what they tell you?"

"No, of course not. I check documents like birth certificates to show their age. The thing is, Mr. Macalvie, there are a lot of lonely men around and—"

He interrupted. "I know, but their company should not be sixteen-year-old girls. My guess is the one sitting down the bar there managed to use somebody else's birth certificate."

Honey slipped from the stool and walked down the bar. Macalvie watched as she talked to the girl and the man sitting there, who, after she left them, got off their bar stools, went over to the dance floor, and started dancing.

Macalvie noticed they didn't look particularly upset or irritated, so he assumed Honey must be one hell of a diplomat.

Now she came back and said, "Are you satisfied?" He didn't answer. "Just what sort of work do you do, Mr. Macalvie?"

"I'm a cop."

"You don't look like the local police. I'm familiar with them."

He laughed. "I bet you are. Not in that way."

"So, where are you?"

"I work in Exeter, and yes, before you tell me I have no authority here, you are absolutely right. There's not a thing I can do to you, even if I find what you're telling me isn't the whole truth."

"I do not know the whole truth about anything, and neither do you."

"Right. I was just wondering about what happened afterwards," said Macalvie.

"After what?"

"After your dancing hostesses leave for the night? Do they meet up with anyone outside of the dance hall?"

"No, they're not supposed to do that."

"Are you sure they pay attention to this rule?"

"Well, if they don't, they get fired. And it's true I did have to let one girl go because she was seeing one of the men in here."

"Betty Jean—you said she was going to Brighton, and you weren't really sure if she was going alone."

Honey thought about this. "That's true. That's because this man had come in here quite a lot, and Betty Jean was his favorite."

"You don't know if she left with him?"

"No. I didn't see them leave together."

Macalvie took out his money clip, slammed down a ten-quid note on the bar, and said, "Honey, thank you very much. You have helped a lot."

"I hope you will be back for another tango, Mac."

"I will. Now I must collect my sergeant and take off for Brighton."

He left the bar. Macalvie almost hated to interrupt Wiggins and the woman who was enveloping him in her arms, but not quite. He broke them up.

"Okay, twinkle toes. Time to go."

Wiggins looked sorely disappointed but apologized to whatever-her-name-was and left with Macalvie.

"Brighton?"

"Yes. As far as Honey knows, this is where she went."

"Okay. How far is it from here?"

"Maybe two hours."

"You got sisters or brothers?" asked Wiggins as they drove along and passed the sign for the A35.

"No. Sorry, Wiggins. That just runs the gamut of siblings. I do not have either one."

"You are an only child?"

"That's right."

"Your mother? Father?"

"Dead."

Wiggins was lost in all his questions, so Macalvie gave him some free information.

"No. I have never been married. No girlfriend, mate, or any kind of partner."

"Honey seemed to enjoy your company."

"For the ten minutes it took to get through that dance. You trying to fix me up, Wiggins?"

"Oh, no. It just seems to me you are kind of alone."

"That's right. Like half of the population in the world."

Macalvie was quiet for a while, then he said, "That was not always the case. There was someone once, named Maggie. I lived with her for two years. She had a little girl, Cassie. One night Cassie was abducted from her bed."

"Oh my God."

"It was three days before we heard anything, and you can imagine what those three days were like, Wiggins. I got a note telling me to go to this place called Fleet Valley, and I realized this was the revenge for my having been the head of a team of men responsible for the shooting of this guy's little girl. I oversaw this team. This was his way of getting back at me. So I went to the place they asked me to go to. It was an old, run-down farmhouse. I went inside and into the kitchen. Cassie was sitting on a chair at a table, with a bowl of cereal in front of her. She was dead. She had been shot in the head."

"My God."

"I was absolutely— I cannot describe the way I felt. I had to go back and tell Maggie what had happened. It was unbelievable. That is what it was. And of course, Maggie and I separated because she could not stand living with me, since she unconsciously blamed me. I never saw her again. So if you are wondering why I am alone, that's the reason, Wiggins."

Wiggins heard what lay underneath Macalvie's voice.

A few hours later, they were in Brighton scouring the streets for a guesthouse called Lavender's. They were sitting in the car on the road above the wide shell beach. Macalvie grunted and put the car in gear as if he wanted to go anyplace at all.

Wiggins turned to him and entered into his own feelings enough to say, "I loathe this place. I've always loathed it."

"But it's known for the brilliance of its air, Wiggins. Nobody loathes Brighton. Nobody."

"The brilliance of its air, but I don't see much of that reflected on those huge waves slapping against the shore."

"Well, if that isn't a testament to otherworldliness, I don't know what is."

"Ha," said Wiggins. "The sea air is bad for you. I don't care what anybody says. It is bad for you." Wiggins snuffled. Got out his handkerchief as if to demonstrate the badness.

"It's your mission that brought us here."

They did not find Lavender's, and finally Wiggins pulled up to the curb and went into the first of hundreds of B and Bs to find the location. Wiggins spoke to a woman behind a reception desk.

She said, "Oh, yes. Lily Lavender. Just go on Atlingworth Street, drive along for a bit, and look over towards the coast, and you will see this long, colorful house with window boxes, gardens, signs. Like I said, you cannot miss it."

"Thanks very much." He got into the car and told Macalvie.

It was certainly true. After driving a quarter of a mile along the coast, they could not miss it. It might as well have been painted from a kid's paintbox. The sign itself was bright purple, and it said LAVENDER'S.

# 36

The wooden sign also bore the name of the proprietor, Winnie Lavender. If this was Winnie who opened the door to them, she looked very much like a Winifred—Wiggins could not imagine calling her Winnie. She was tall, slender, and pleasant-looking, but with a sharp nose and chin.

"Mrs. Lavender?" said Wiggins, who automatically took out his ID and showed it to her.

Macalvie just leaned against the door frame and waited for the expected "Police? Why are the police coming here?"

"Mrs. Lavender, we are just trying to get a little information about one of your guests, or at least a person who once was a guest here. That would be my sister, Betty Jean Wiggins. Is that name familiar at all to you?"

Breaking down and inviting them inside, she said, "Oh yes. Of course. Betty Jean has been living here for over a year now."

"Do you know where she is now?" asked Wiggins.

"Well, she is at work. She works as a server. Or she might be with her man friend, Mr. Leder."

Both Macalvie and Wiggins stopped in their tracks. "Did you say Leder?" said Wiggins. "Could it be Leder*er*?"

"Well, I guess it could be, but I think it's just Leder."

"Does Mr. Leder have a first name?"

"He does. I am not sure what it is. John? Something like that."

"You wouldn't happen to know where this Leder guy lives, would you?"

"No, as far as I know he's just another tourist."

"But you referred to him as her man friend, which suggests a kind of standing relationship."

"That I wouldn't know about," said Mrs. Lavender. "I know that he saw her a number of times while she was here. That is why I referred to him as BJ's man friend."

"Where is this place?" asked Macalvie, holding up a blank order pad. At the top it said MINNIE MOUSE CAFÉ.

"Oh that," said Mrs. Lavender. "It's just a couple of blocks down there, left-hand side, on the corner. A cute little place."

"Thanks very much, Mrs. Lavender," said Wiggins. "You have been an immense help."

Out on the porch again, Mac and Wiggins looked off to the left and to the right, as if Betty Jean might come walking up to the house.

"Okay. Where now?" said Wiggins.

Macalvie held up the order pad. "To the Minnie Mouse Café, of course."

They both left and headed for the Minnie Mouse Café. And there she was. Wiggins could not believe it. There was his sister, BJ. After five years. And she had barely changed at all. She was standing with one of the same order pads that Macalvie had found, by a table of what looked to be truck drivers or construction workers, and she turned from the table and saw Wiggins. She stood there frozen for a minute. And so did Wiggins. And then she went loose, her feet started to move, and she ran to him.

"Al, Alfie, where did you come from?" She threw her arms around him, and Wiggins grabbed onto her and said, "From the B and B up the street where you're living."

Standing at the counter, Macalvie had watched BJ running toward Wiggins, calling his name, and weeping. He watched the two of them for a minute, then he went up to the bar, got a Glenlivet for himself, and brought it back to the table where Wiggins and BJ were now sitting. "Now, I hope you covered five years while I was gone so I don't have to listen to it."

"Oh, come on, sir," said Wiggins. "Look, you've gone to all this trouble. You have gone from Cornwall to Lyme Regis to Brighton, and you're pretending you aren't interested?"

"It is no pretense. It is going to be some kind of long pseudo-sad story of Ms. Betty Jean Wiggins, who was unhappy at home, escaped by the back door, went around to the front, met up with her sleezy boyfriend, and took off."

"Well," said BJ, "if you already know the story, why am I here telling it?"

"Not for my benefit," said Macalvie. "It is for your brother, whom you have ignored for all these years."

"It seems to me," said BJ, "you're not really asking for me to go over what happened, because you already seem to know that. What you want me to do is to explain why it happened. Unfortunately, I'm not really sure myself why it happened. It's just the way I felt at the time, and it's probably the only explanation I can give you."

"Okay, BJ. Then I guess it's time to leave," said Macalvie.

BJ looked at Macalvie with a question on her face. "Leave?"

"Go back to your digs and collect your stuff and be on our way."

"On our way where, Mr. Macalvie?"

"Manchester."

BJ looked from him to her brother. "We are going to Manchester, Alfie?"

"You're going home, BJ," said Wiggins.

"But—"

"No buts, BJ. Mum really wants to see you, and I think you want to see her."

"I do."

"So let's go," said Wiggins.

They went back to Lavender's. It took no time at all for BJ to collect her belongings and stow them in Macalvie's car. She said a tearful goodbye to Mrs. Lavender and followed Wiggins to the car. Macalvie then said, "Okay, let's go." They pulled away from the curb, and they were off from Brighton to the A30.

Two hours later, Macalvie pulled off the A30 toward Lyme Regis. Wiggins looked at him in surprise. "Why are we going to Lyme Regis?" In another fifteen minutes, Wiggins saw where they were going. "This is Honey's Dance Hall," he said.

"Right. You did not really think I was going to let you or your sister go without having a dance, did you?"

And then Wiggins and BJ saw the white banner fluttering above the porch: WELCOME BACK BETTY JEAN. BJ gasped. "My goodness. What is all this?"

"It is just what it says. Welcome back." They piled out of the car, went up the steps and inside, and were immediately greeted by Honey. Honey and Betty Jean just seemed to float in an embrace, and Wiggins thought the dancing was going to start right there, but it did not. Macalvie pulled Betty Jean away and walked her onto the dance floor to the opening strings of "Moonlight Serenade." There were a number of people on the dance floor who recognized Betty Jean and applauded even before she did anything. Wiggins just stood by stupidly, leaning against the doorjamb and watching the smooth display of Betty Jean and Macalvie, as good a pair as if they were living in each other's pockets.

Wiggins could not believe it, nor could he put up with it for very long. He walked over to them and cut in. "Come on, BJ. Let's show them what dancing is all about."

Wiggins floated her off. She looked, for the first time since he'd seen her, alive, as if all of the energy, all of the grace, all of the perfect timing had returned in a rush. From "Moonlight Serenade" they went into "String of Pearls," and Betty Jean came up with even more enthusiasm. She was challenging Wiggins to go faster. So they whirled and twirled. Finally, as if exhausted from this double dose of flying to the moon, Betty Jean slumped against Wiggins. She said, "Al, that was wonderful."

After an hour at Honey's Dance Hall, they piled back into the car and returned to the A30. They had been on the road for a while when Macalvie turned off.

"Why are we getting off the A30?" said Wiggins.

"That's simple," said Macalvie. "To get to the motorway."

"But that doesn't go to Exeter."

"We're not going to Exeter. Your mum lives in Manchester."

This time it was Betty Jean who interrupted. "But I thought you said we were going to Exeter to get Al's car."

"No, we're going to Manchester."

"But . . ." Wiggins started to say something. "How did my car get to Manchester? I left it in Exeter."

"Wiggins, your deductive powers never cease to amaze me. Your car is in Manchester because I called headquarters and asked one of the guys to take your car to Manchester. It's a hell of a lot quicker if we don't have to go to Cornwall, unless of course your sister wants to see Mousehole again."

Betty Jean laughed, then suddenly she turned quiet and said, weeping, "Poor Mum."

Macalvie turned from the steering wheel and said, "Poor mum? You think your mother is feeling sad?"

"It's going to be such a shock seeing me again."

"Not to her. She knows you're coming. You are going to be the one doing the crying, Betty Jean. You are the one who has been gone for five years."

Wiggins, as if in acknowledgement of this mild rebuke, slid down in her seat and they continued on their way.

When they finally drove up to Wiggins's house, before the car had come to a stop, Betty Jean flung herself out onto the curb and up to the porch, to her mother. "Poor mum," she cried. She stood at the top of the stairs, radiant in smiles. Even Hermione stood beside her, looking as if she might allow the world to continue to live.

Amid many sobs, apologies, and embraces, Wiggins came up and joined his mum and Betty Jean, doubling the enthusiastic joy of the reunion. Then they went into the living room and sat down. Betty Jean and her mum started talking—nothing of real consequence, just a lot of talking about where she had been, where she stayed, and what the weather had been like. All the while, Hermione, who looked as if she could take on the Devon Constabulary single-pawedly, was now leaning against Commander Macalvie as if he too had suddenly come home.

After speaking on his phone to one of his men, he hung up and said, "Sorry, folks, I am going back to Exeter." He pushed the cat from his leg and said, "Sorry, cat."

Hermione glared at him before she jumped onto the floor, looked around the room, did not see anything she liked, and stomped out. Wiggins smiled. She reminded him of Macalvie. Outside the house, Wiggins said, "Commander, how did you do it? How did you get Betty Jean to come home here?"

"Come on, Wiggins, are you blind? She's sick."

Wiggins nearly fell back onto the porch steps. "What?"

"You can't tell? Look at her eyes. They look like cinders. Look at her weight. I don't know what she looked like before, but I am sure she weighed more than she does right now."

"How can you be so sure?"

"Because I am a buffer, Wiggins, and I asked her. She is ashamed. That is the reason she has not been home."

"How did she even have the energy, not to mention the desire, to do all that dancing at Honey's?"

"Because that is what happens. I have seen it in other people. Suddenly you get this surge, or you don't want to use up the little energy you have in being sick. Wiggins, is your conversation going to be limited to how or why? I am glad you're not driving me back to Exeter."

"Mr. Macalvie, when you made these arrangements, you called Mum? You must have done it. Did you tell her?"

"Of course not. That is up to Betty Jean, isn't it? Look, Wiggins, I am sorry your sister is sick. I like Betty Jean. She is a nice woman, and a hell of a good dancer. What is not to like? I am glad I met her and your mother, and God knows I met that cat. Get her to a doctor, he will probably want to run some tests. See you later."

Macalvie went down to the pavement and got into his car. Wiggins stood there as he drove off.

# 37

Jury did not get into Treadnor's house until after the memorial service. Alice could not have been home very long when he went into the living room. She was seated on one of the twin couches. The tissues on the coffee table attested to a bit, if not a lot, of weeping. He apologized for bothering her at this time. She merely raised her eyes and lowered them.

"I'm sorry, Alice. This is not a good time."

"Go ahead, ask away. It won't be easier tomorrow or the next day," said Alice.

"This Jason Lederer. He might be the man who was shot at the Queen, Alice."

She gasped as she fell back against the sofa. "I don't know

what you are talking about. As I told you, the man who was shot was my husband!"

Jury thought her surprise didn't include much in the way of relief. He said so. "But I'd think you'd be happy to accept the fact that your husband hadn't been shot."

She sighed heavily and looked everywhere but at Jury. "Of course I'd be happy, if I could believe it. But then, where in God's name *is* Tom?" She stared at the door as if he might appear.

"We don't know," said Jury. He added, "I was wondering, Alice, if you had an attorney?"

"An attorney? Yes. Of course. It's the law firm called Wootton and Scarsdale. They're in the city. They've been the Treadnors' attorneys for as long as I can remember, so I am assuming they would handle anything that has to do with this."

Jury thought for a moment then reached into an inner pocket and pulled out a little stack of cards. He extracted one and handed it to Alice.

"Who's this?" she asked.

"The best attorney in London," answered Jury.

Looking at the card, she said, "Pete Apted? Q.C.? He's only interested in defending the Queen."

Jury said, "He takes other cases if he finds them troubled enough."

"That's what you think mine is?"

"I'd say shooting someone sitting at a bar through a window might qualify for Pete Apted. The only problem is that he is extremely busy. He's got so many dockets on his desk, he's taken half of them off to use as a footstool."

"He sounds interesting," said Alice.

"Oh, he's interesting all right. Another problem is that you'll have to talk to him."

"You see that as a problem?"

Jury smiled. "I can set you up an interview."

# 38

"Drop me off in Mayfair," said Jury as they drove along the Thames toward the bridge.

"Mr. Plant's club?"

"Yes. If they'll let me in."

"Oh, surely by now they know you."

"That's the problem." Jury laughed.

"He hasn't come down, sir," said the little gnome of a porter. "Shall I call him and let him know you're here?"

"Oh, by no means. I'll just wait for him in there." Jury nodded toward the Members' Room, in which a dozen or so members sat in varying degrees of reduced consciousness. Somnolence? Coma? Death?

"Certainly, sir. I'll just let Lord Ardry know when he comes down where you are."

"I expect he'll recognize me."

The porter gave a creaky laugh.

"Superintendent!" called out Colonel Neame from where he sat with Major Champs, one on either side of the fireplace. "Join us, please! Have a whiskey."

"Just what I was planning to do." Jury removed his coat and dropped it over the back of a sofa, from which it was quickly gathered up by a porter and whisked away to a mysterious cupboard somewhere.

"Are you on a case here?" asked Colonel Neame, seemingly hopeful. Ever since the murder a couple of years ago when someone had walked in with a knife and stabbed one of the members in the heart, Colonel Neame and Major Champs always seemed to hope it would happen again.

"No, just browsing, Major."

They both thought that was hysterically funny and laughed and slapped the arms of their chairs.

A tray of fresh drinks had arrived and so had Melrose Plant, who helped himself to one, the one being Jury's, of course.

"Hey, that's mine!"

"You've already had one. I haven't."

"Get your own."

The porter, still standing there and enjoying this little contretemps, said, "Not to worry. I'll get yours, Lord Ardrey. I'll get a fresh bottle of something better—" Then, realizing that Colonel Neame and Major Champs would not appreciate having got something worse, he said, "How about a fresh bottle of an eighteen-year-old Glenlivet?"

"I'd take an eighteen-minute-old Glenlivet at this point, thanks."

"Fresh bottle?" said Major Champs. "I doubt that Glenlivet would be able to sit around long enough to go stale." Champs chortled at his own little joke.

The porter made his exit, and Colonel Neame said, "I'm starving; come on, Champs. They're having chateaubriand tonight." He turned to Melrose and Jury. "I don't suppose you'd care to join us?"

"Thank you, Colonel, but no. I think we'll toss down a few more before we go in."

"Just don't eat all of the chateaubriand," said Jury.

After they'd left, Melrose said, "You seem to be especially sunk into some kind of grim mental state."

"Don't be dramatic. I'm just thinking of Alice Treadnor's behavior when I went to the house after the memorial service."

"But after all, her husband was murdered. She'd just come back from the service. Why would you expect she'd react as usual?"

"Because people do. Basic behaviors don't change much. One might be extremely upset, hysterical, badly depressed—all sorts of things; but events don't change underlying behaviors." Jury frowned.

"Is that significant?"

"Yes. She didn't make a Manhattan."

"A Manhattan?"

"Her favorite drink. Her *only* drink. The one she was making the first time I went to the house. She never misses a cocktail hour."

"But this was right after the memorial service, so surely she might have put it off then."

Jury shook his head. "I've missed trains, planes, and appointments. I've missed weddings and funerals. But I've never missed a cocktail hour."

"You think she'll be arrested?"

Jury nodded.

"A decent prosecutor would tear this whole story to ribbons. You do realize that," said Melrose.

"Certainly, a prosecutor could tear this story apart, but I don't think it would be all that easy."

"Oh, come on, Jury. Maybe your reasoning in this case is being clouded because you're damn attracted to Alice Treadnor. You just can't think straight."

"Don't be ridiculous, Plant! My emotions have nothing to do with it." Jury drank the rest of his whiskey.

Melrose said, "Well I assume she's got a very good defense attorney."

Jury said, "She will. Pete Apted."

Melrose looked at him in astonishment. "Pete Apted? Apted wouldn't take on this bunch of, excuse me, swill."

Jury laughed. "If it is swill, Apted would love it all the more. He's very attracted to swill."

"The trust itself is in the hands of the bank. Well, those hands are the hands of people. So, could Treadnor have gotten to one of those people and arranged for the trust to come into someone else's hands? If his own couldn't do it?"

"A bank? I hardly think so. If the trust were to be accessible, it would be in some other way."

"Well, it seems the only people who would have access according to the will would be Alice and Ross. And you don't appear to think it was Ross, despite his broken alibi. So, what's going to happen now."

Jury shrugged. "I think she'll be arrested."

"Soon?"

Jury nodded.

"I assume the Treadnors have a lawyer."

At that moment, the porter entered with one of the house phones. "Lord Ardry, a call for you."

"This is so unusual," Melrose started. "For me? Who?"

"I believe the gentleman said he was your butler."

Melrose grabbed the receiver. "Ruthven? Is there an emergency?"

Ruthven answered that there wasn't. But something important had happened that he was sure his lordship would want to see.

"See? See what?"

It was something Ruthven would prefer not to describe over the phone, given its unusual nature.

"Oh, come on, Ruthven. You're keeping me in too much suspense."

Ruthven sighed and told him that, to put his lordship's mind at ease, he would simply tell him it was something that fell off the back of a truck.

"The back of a truck! And that's supposed to ease my mind? What was it? A cartload of corn? A shipment of rifles for the IRA? Is there still an IRA?"

Ruthven sighed again and said he knew he shouldn't have told him anything, as it was only making things worse. Though when his lordship saw it, all would appear perfectly simple to him. More or less. Ruthven apologized and said it would be best if Lord Ardry simply returned to Ardry End—although there was no hurry. They rang off.

"What was that all about?"

"How would I know? He wouldn't tell me."

"Something fell off the back of a truck?"

"Probably Agatha."

# 39

"*This*," said Melrose, "could not have fallen off the back of a truck!"

"Oh, but it did, sir!"

"It certainly did; I saw it!"

"It was as I told you, m'lord—"

These various responses were offered by the several members of the staff gathered round in the back near the barn.

"It's a goat," said Melrose. "A goat."

"Indeed, it is, m'lord. When Martha and I were out here seeing to Aggrieved, Gerrard being God knows where." Seldom did Ruthven allow himself to stoop to such expressions, but Gerrard was a constant irritant, it seemed. Ruthven went on: "A truck drove by in the Northampton Road"—and here he paused to indicate the road, as if Melrose might have forgotten during his time at Boring's—"presumably carrying livestock, as I can't imagine it would be only the one goat, and suddenly—"

Martha horned in here: "The back flew open, and the goat flew out!"

Melrose did not take this literally.

"So here we were, and the goat down there in the road," said Ruthven. "Well, I felt we had to see to it. And we righted it—it was lying on its side—and led it up here."

"With the intention of doing what?"

"Well, we don't rightly know, do we, m'lord? We were waiting for you to get back."

"But that was last night, Martha. I mean, what did you do with it in the meantime?"

"Stood around talking about the poor goat, that was probably lamed by the fall, like we're doing now." This little outburst, to everyone's astonishment, was delivered by Pippen, who never expressed herself, she being the youngest and most recent addition to the staff, and thus most likely to be the target of outbursts rather than the initiator of them. Then she came to herself, adjusted her cap, looked frightenedly around as if the air were her enemy, bowed slightly in no special direction, and begged pardon.

Melrose said, "Absolutely, Pippen. You're quite right. This standing about is largely my fault, as I was taken so much by surprise. Tell you what: Why don't we put you in charge of the goat. You can see if you think it needs medical attention—that one leg doesn't look quite the ticket. You can see to its being fed and brushed and generally taken care of."

Even the goat looked as though it would like to return Melrose's dazzling smile, for all the others did, without the dazzle.

Pippen herself looked more than relieved. She looked as if she might grow wings and fly off to goat land. "Oh, yes, sir; I'll take perfect care of her. Shall we give her a name?"

Melrose was about to speak, when a voice behind them spoke for him. "What—"

He turned. Agatha stood there, staring with her mouth open.

"Agape," he said. "That's the new name, Pippen: Agape!"

"Agape and Aghast! What could be better?"

A number of things, apparently, as Agatha was prepared to go on with them. "You've got a goat!"

What a marvelous statement to take out of context: "You've got a goat." He'd love to hear it repeated all up and down the M1. "You've got a goat, you've got a goat, you've got a goat."

"That's right, Agatha. Now, why else are you here?"

"Well, I'm not here for the goat! Why on earth did you find it necessary to get another goat?"

More raucous laughter up and down the M1.

"You've already got a goat!" She said this reprovingly.

As if he were only allowed one. "I've already got an aunt, too."

Agatha looked around wildly, as if aunts proliferated near the barn, just like goats. "What on earth are you talking about?"

"Not here, but in London. You remember the Gerrards of London?" Melrose loved saying this, as if the Gerrards of London were lent some sort of sweeping nobility by the repetition of the name.

"You mean that boy who was here?"

"And still is, Agatha. And as he's my cousin, his mother would be an aunt." How did he reckon this, for heaven's sake? She was somebody's aunt, but hardly his. He dropped this subject and said, "Mr. Blodgett, would you kindly go and find Aghast?" "Find" was overstating it, since Aghast was either in the barn, chewing away at whatever Blodgett had given him, or out here, chewing away at whatever Ardry End had on offer.

Now here was Aghast being led by Blodgett on a thin rope that he twitched now and again, as if leading the goat past the review stand at the Westminster Dog Show.

Melrose was immensely pleased that Aghast took to Agape as if they were old buddies.

Pippen looked even more pleased. "Would you look at that, sir? It's as if this little goat came out of a past the two of them shared."

Agatha looked almost as surprised by Pippen's addressing Melrose as she had been by the appearance of the second goat.

And to add to that surprise, a voice resonated in the twilight. "Two goats?" said Jury, who'd come up behind them. "One wasn't enough? Aren't you ever satisfied?"

"Jury! How did you get here?"

"Fell off the back of a truck."

They sat in the library, Agatha having taken herself off for once of her own accord, "to dine," she said, "with Lambert."

"Dine?" asked Melrose. "Where? Are there actually dining establishments around here? The Blue Parrot? The Sidbury Old Oak Tearoom?"

After the stormy, or rather, stumpy departure of Agatha, they settled back with their drinks. Melrose said, "Let's go back to Alice Treadnor and her uncharacteristic behavior."

"That's right. It wasn't his death that put her off it. I think something ominous must have come to mind that drove out everything else."

"She couldn't have been upset by the service?"

"No. We just discussed that." Jury set his drink on the side table and sat forward. "Here's what I'm thinking: Perhaps it occurred to her that her husband might simply not come back. Oh, he'd have come back to London, of course, to see to his inheritance. To do whatever needed doing in order to collect that trust money. But what if he didn't go back to *her*? There was talk about his wanting a divorce. Alice told me that."

"But if she got the goods from Tom's will, that would have included the trust fund—yes, I know, she couldn't touch it herself, but wouldn't he need to get her to give it up from their own inheritance?"

"I don't think so. Not the way Treadnor Senior had it written."

"So you think she's going to be arrested?"

"I do."

"And will Pete Apted take this case?"

"Don't know."

"But isn't this Twickenham police's case?"

"Yes. But they're part of the Met, and for some reason, the Commissioner wants the Yard to do this. Ridiculous."

# 40

"Another goat? You're kidding!" said Marshall Trueblood.

"I wish he were," said Jury, taking a place on the window seat beside Vivian.

"That means another name-finding contest. All right . . ." Trueblood looked around for something to write on. "Now, how many of us are there?"

Jury rolled his eyes. As if it ever changed.

Trueblood was pointing his finger, apparently actually counting. "That's five."

"You can't count this little group around this table?" said Jury. "There're six."

"Forgot myself."

"I'm in!" said Mrs. Withersby, who wasn't actually one of those at the table. "I got me name all ready."

"How could you? We only just found out there was another goat."

Jury made a sound in his throat. Could anyone say that without swallowing his tongue? "Mrs. Withersby can have my place. I'm all out of goat suggestions."

"At times," said Trueblood, "I think you want to take the fun out of things."

"No, I just want to take the goat out of things."

Trueblood gave him a dirty look and went on handing the napkins around. "What time limit shall we put on this?"

"A month?" said Jury.

Joanna Lewes, who didn't want to take away more time than necessary from her manuscript, said, "Five minutes, how about that?"

"Have you actually got a stopwatch, Trueblood?" he said, seeing Marshall set before him what looked like one.

"I always carry it."

They bit on pencils, stared into the air.

"I've got mine!" said Mrs. Withersby, tossing her bit of paper onto the table.

"Withers, you're supposed to keep it to yourself until we all finish."

"Agony! It meets all the rules. Got to begin with an *A-G*."

"But that's the name you gave to the first goat!"

Jury squinched his eyes shut. Had someone really said that?

"Okay, your turn, Dianne."

"Agree." Dianne looked around for applause. None was forthcoming.

Trueblood nodded toward Vivian.

"Again."

That earned her an inappreciative stare.

"Joanna?"

"Agatha!"

The door had just opened, and Melrose's aunt came in.

She stood staring round the table for a moment, until Melrose said, "Agatha! You look absolutely awful. Is something wrong? You're absolutely ag—" He almost said it, but took it back.

"It's Lambert!"

Trueblood looked expectant. "Oh, has he been hit by the milk truck?"

"Kindly don't sound so hopeful, Mr. Trueblood. No, it's not him; it's that snake, Theo—"

"Theo got hit?"

"Don't be ridiculous. No. Theo Wrenn Browne is suing Lambert for theft! That appalling Browne has already called the police!"

"Called the police? But why? We've already got the police right here!"

Agatha looked stupidly round the room. "Here? Where? I don't see—"

Jury raised his hand.

"Oh, you. No. I mean *real* police—"

Vivian rose from the window seat. "Agatha! How can you possibly refer to Superintendent Jury as not a real policeman? You should be ashamed of—"

Quickly, Agatha switched from outrage to simper: "Oh, do forgive me, Superintendent! I didn't mean to offend you. Heavens, you're just too much one of us to be taken as an *unfamiliar*."

Jury held out his hand. "No apology necessary, Lady Ardry."

She fairly bloomed at being addressed with her nonexistent title. "You've just been here so often in this room, in Ardry End, in—"

Again, Jury tried to shut her up with the hand gesture. "Just what is it that Strether is alleged to have stolen?"

"A Henry James novel. The first edition of *The Ambassadors*. It's absurd, of course! Theo claims he took it because it was the book in which Lambert Strether starred."

"Starred!" Trueblood laughed.

"I'm surprised," said Melrose. "Theo has a first edition? Where in hell did he get it?"

Joanne Lewes looked up from her notebook to say, "Are you sure it's 'edition' he's talking about and not 'printing'? A first edition of James would be extremely valuable and hard to come by. But there could be many printings. My last book has gone through a dozen printings—God knows why—but no second edition. I mean, something that would mean changes have been made. In that book, why would anyone bother? But given the books are popular—" Here she shrugged another "God knows why." "And what first edition is Theo claiming it is? That in itself should be interesting." She looked at Agatha. "Where's your friend Lambert right now?"

"At the shop. Arguing with that snake Theo!"

Jury got up. "Perhaps I'll go and have a word."

From the street, they could hear the raised voices inside the Wrenn's Nest.

"Mr. Browne! Mr. Strether!" said Jury. "Perhaps you could stop long enough to tell us exactly what's happened with Henry James."

Theo went right to it: "This book is what he tried to put in place of my first edition! Imagine!"

"Where did you get James's first edition?"

Theo shrugged slightly. "In a job lot of books. I picked it up at one of Christie's auctions."

"That would have been almost accidental, Mr. Browne. And what did you do with your copy, Mr. Strether?"

"I simply laid it on the counter."

"Where did you get this, Mr. Strether? Why would you have a first edition on your shelf? I would think such a book would be tucked away behind the desk. Where is it now?"

Strether looked angry. "Well, he must have it!"

"Well, when you do turn it up, Mr. Browne, I'd like to see it. I doubt the first edition ever existed. Number one, Christie's would never toss such a remarkable book into a 'job lot' of other books. I wouldn't have put it on the shelf. The two books—your first edition and Mr. Strether's book—didn't look at all alike, so why don't we forget the whole thing?"

Jury placed his notebook in his pocket.

# 41

Back from the goat-naming jamboree, Jury and Melrose were relaxing by his fire, talking about goats, goat-naming, and of course, Agatha. Suddenly Jury remembered Benny Keagan, got up, and said, "I've got to go back to London. Where's Wiggins? He's supposed to be back from his trip to Manchester."

Melrose inclined his head toward the stable—barn, really, but Ruthven liked to call it a stable. Indeed, Ruthven had walked into the living room at that moment and said, "Is there anything I can do for you, Superintendent?"

"There is," said Jury. "Would you go out to the stable and tell Wiggins to go around to the car, and I'll meet him there."

"Certainly, sir." Ruthven left.

"Why do you have to go back to London? It's nearly dinnertime. We were just having predinner drinks."

"I've got to see to some business."

"Oh, you. Scotland Yard. Oh, sure."

"I'll talk to you later." He turned and left, then walked to the car where Wiggins was now standing.

"What's up, boss? Why do we have to go back to London?"

"Well, we do live there, Wiggins. We do work there, remember?"

"No, no, no, I mean, right now."

They were both in the car and Jury said, "I remembered that Benny Keagan needed me to do something."

"Benny? What's going on with Benny?"

"There's always something going on with Benny. In any event, I want to find him. So let's go."

"But where to? You don't know where Benny is. He's always working."

"Yeah, he'll be making deliveries. So the first place we can make a stop is at Gyp's."

"Gyp the butcher? That awful man?"

"Okay, Wiggins. Let's go."

After less than an hour on the road, Wiggins pulled the car up in front of Gyp's store. Jury got out, walked in the front door, and found the shop empty. He walked through it and out the back door. Wiggins followed. They came upon a scene that was ludicrous and horrible. They saw a piglet running this way and that, zigzagging all over the backyard, while Gyp the butcher was chasing the piglet with a huge knife. The piglet is running for its life, thought Jury as it smashed up against his leg. Jury picked the piglet up.

"Okay, Gyp. That's all. That is all."

Jury handed the piglet to Wiggins and said, "Take the pig back to the barn."

Wiggins took the piglet and walked back to a small barn whose doors were closed.

Jury said, "Gyp, I think this might just be the end of you."

"What are you talking about? How dare you walk onto this property! How dare you threaten me! How dare you take my pig!" As Jury was about to answer this charge, Wiggins yelled from the barn, "Sir, you've got to see this."

Jury left Gyp and walked back to the barn. "What?" he said.

"Just come on, look!"

Wiggins had opened the main barn door. Blood. It wasn't visible, but the air was suffused with it. Jury looked in and saw a big meat-chopping block, much larger than the ones ordinarily seen in kitchens. On the back of this block, there were slits for knives. A number of different knives were in them. Jury looked beyond this butcher's block and saw a long table, on which were small cages. He counted ten cages, each with a piglet inside it. Then right above that was a slightly taller table, and that had three cages on it, two of them with piglets, the third empty. Jury looked at Wiggins, who was still clutching the piglet that had been running across the yard.

Wiggins said, "Have you ever seen anything like it?"

Jury said, "No. I hope it's not what I think it is."

"Well, it is. What Gyp is doing is slaughtering a piglet, and all the others around are the audience. The audience, sir! Can you imagine?"

Jury just stood there staring, horrified. And then he said, "*Heart of Darkness*, Wiggins."

"What's that?"

"A remarkable story by Joseph Conrad. I'm thinking of it because one of the characters was a man named Kurtz. Totally evil amongst cannibals in the Congo. Gyp is our Kurtz, Wiggins, and he's not going to be doing this again." Jury slammed the barn door closed, and since there wasn't a lock, he jammed a stick in between the catch and the handle. "Okay, Wiggins. Get me Karl Mundt."

"Who's Karl Mundt, sir?"

"He's with the RSPCA, and he is in charge of one particular part of it that deals with animal abuse. Here, give me the phone. I'll get him."

"Yes, sir."

Jury looked in his small address book and got the number for Karl Mundt. It rang several times before someone picked it up.

"Mundt."

"Hello, Mr. Mundt. I don't know if you remember me, but my name is Jury."

"You're the Scotland Yard guy. Sure, I remember. What can I do for you?"

Jury explained the piglet situation in Gyp's barn and filled Mundt in on how Gyp dealt with the pigs.

"What a creep," said Mundt.

Jury said, "I just thought you might have some ideas as to how I could handle this."

Mundt said, "Well, there are a lot of city codes about animal abuse. I recently finished with one case where a guy named Rico Barnes violated every single code."

"So you were able to nab him?"

"Well, not exactly. It's very hard to get proof when it comes to animal abuse. But it happens I know a guy who has a parcel of land near Huddersfield he's turned into a pig sanctuary. He's crazy about pigs."

Jury said, "So I guess they don't wind up getting slaughtered."

"No, indeed," said Mundt. "But I am thinking he might take in some of the piglets. How many did you say there were?"

"About ten or twelve."

"I think Joe would have room for that. His name is Joe Blyth."

Jury said, after a pause, "I met this guy, didn't I, Karl? Wasn't he involved in the dogfighting in the basement of that pub on Hester Street?"

"Yes, he was," said Mundt.

"Did you take any of them in?"

"You can imagine how many eyewitnesses are going to step up and tell a judge what they saw."

"What can I do in this situation?"

"Is this guy giving you a lot of trouble?"

"He's effing and blinding about his civil rights and says there's nothing police can do to him because he has a license for his slaughter operation. Right now, we've got the barn door locked and Wiggins is inside shooting anyone who tries to get through."

"Okay, you probably don't have a search warrant or any piece of paper which allows you to take over these pigs."

"Right," said Jury. "I have nothing."

Mundt said, "Just see if you can shut this guy up for a few hours and I'll ring Joe and see if he can get there this evening."

Jury said, "The only problem is going to be transport. But I think the Yard may have a vehicle."

Mundt interrupted and said, "You don't have to worry about that. Joe has his own transport. He's got two trucks that are always fitted out for rescue operations. Let me give Joe a call and I'll call you right back."

"Thank you," said Jury, and he rang off. He headed for the barn.

He opened the door and walked in. Wiggins was watching the pigs and turned suddenly and saw Jury.

"Boss," he said, "all these pigs look to be all right. Gyp was banging on the door a while ago, but I just ignored it. So what do we do?"

Jury said, "We wait for a call from Karl Mundt."

Jury's phone rang. It was Mundt saying to Jury, "We're in luck. Joe was there and he's getting one of his trucks to drive to Huddersfield. Incidentally, I forgot to tell you this pig-raising business is something Blyth started after he gave up his other work."

"Which was?"

"Oh, he's a contract killer."

"I'm a cop. I can't stand by and watch any kind of killing."

"No, no, no," said Mundt. "Joe doesn't have to kill someone to get their attention. It'll take him about three hours to make the trip. Can you keep this Gyp person in tow for that long?"

"I'm sure we can," said Jury. "Thanks very much."

Jury turned and walked back into Gyp's butcher shop, where Gyp was now taking out his fury on Benny Keagan. "This is that brat's fault. He's the one who did this! He's the one who reported it. I know he is. I'll have the Social on him in five minutes."

"No. I don't think you will, Mr. Gyp. There will be people in your barn. Maybe in under five minutes."

Benny was clearly thrilled to see Jury.

"Mr. Jury! Mr. Jury! Mr. Gyp here says there are police all over the place, but I didn't see any. Mr. Gyp is claiming I had something to do with this, but I don't know what this is. I'm just here to pick up whatever packages Mr. Gyp has for me to deliver. He says he's calling the Social."

"He can call them all he wants, but he can't do anything. All we have to do now is wait for help." Two hours later, help appeared in the form of a flatbed truck nearly a block long. The door opened. Out stepped a tall, blond guy who looked more like a soccer coach than anyone who had anything to do with animals.

Benny was up out of his chair like a shot. Sparky sat at attention, growling in his throat when he saw Gyp.

Jury extended his hand and said, "Richard Jury. CID Scotland Yard. You're Mr. Blyth."

Joe Blyth nodded and said, "Karl filled me in on what sounds like a nasty operation."

Gyp turned his fury on Joe Blyth. "What the hell do you think you're doing here?"

"Well," said Joe, "I understand you have at least ten or twelve piglets in your barn which you mean to butcher."

"They're my property. It's my barn. And there isn't one fucking thing you can do about it."

Something whizzed through the air. Gyp clapped the side of his face and turned to stare at the small knife that was quivering in the wall molding.

"What the hell is this? I'm calling the cops."

"The cops are right here," said Jury. "Nothing has happened to you."

Joe Blyth took out a packet of cigarettes and passed it around to Jury, who looked at them as if they were the last cigarettes on earth.

"I stopped," he said.

"Okay, Mr. Gyp. We have a proposal. You give up the pigs, and Scotland Yard will give you a receipt, and we'll turn the whole thing over to the magistrate."

"You can't do that," yelled Gyp.

"Well, maybe not," said Joe. "Let's just talk about it."

Again, something whizzed through the air, and Gyp clamped his hand on the other side of his face.

"Come on, Gyp," said Joe. "I want to see this operation of yours."

The four of them—or really five if you counted Sparky—then trooped out to the barn.

Jury was saying, "It's a disgrace," as he opened the door. There were twelve cages with one pig each and two empty cages.

Finally, Gyp said, "I'm taking this to court."

Jury said, "I hope so. You've got it set up so the piglets in the cages are around a butcher's block. They are the audience for your butchery."

Gyp sputtered and muttered, but it did not keep them from loading the cages onto Joe's truck, which he had backed up in the alley between the butcher shop and an antique store.

They got all the cages onto the truck. The truck was fitted

out with grass along one side, a narrow trough on the other, and buckets of water.

Joe started letting the pigs out of the cages. The first thing they did was poop on the grass. Finally, Jury said, "Wiggins, you're still holding on to that piglet. You'll have to let it go."

Almost reluctantly, Wiggins turned the piglet over to Joe Blyth.

Fortunately, Wiggins had not noticed that the piglet in its contempt had pooped on his shirt. Jury went over to where Gyp was jumping up and down in some sort of Gyp-against-the-world calisthenics. He grabbed the towel off his arm, went back to Wiggins, and said, "Here, Wiggins, just clean that up."

Jury and Joe talked briefly about pigs before Joe climbed up into the truck and started the engine. Jury followed the truck out of the driveway onto the circular road, where he stood and watched it departing. He saw the faces of two of the pigs that had managed to climb on top of their cages and were staring out the rear-door window of the truck. Jury patted his pockets for cigarettes, the way he used to do in moments of stress or loss or some other uncomfortable feeling, before he realized he had stopped smoking years before and dropped his hands. He watched the piglets go as the vehicle disappeared around the corner, and thought about Carole-anne's fry-ups.

He felt a double loss.

No more cigarettes.

No more sausages.

# 42

"I know this is a kind of hell, Alice," said Jury, sitting across from her where she was drinking a baroque Manhattan. "I know it's hellish." "Opaque" was the word Brad Ross had used to describe her. Her expression right now was not calm, but still. Why was he sitting here making these fine distinctions instead of finishing his sentence, instead of telling her what he'd come for. "*But* . . ."

"What?" she said. "What is it you're trying to tell me?"

"That I think you're going to be arrested, Alice, for the murder of Jason Lederer."

She sighed, then got up suddenly and went to the fireplace and rested her hand against the mantle.

"That's absolutely ridiculous. You heard me say I was here all evening. All night—"

He interrupted. "That's part of the evidence you presented, but it's only circumstantial. All of the points in your alibi, Alice, are circumstantial."

"I must have seen everyone who works here for a little while. I told you. I told the police. I talked to Alan. I talked to Santos, and the maid. I talked to everyone."

She turned away from the fireplace and stared at him.

"I know you did." Jury paused. "All I'm telling you is there's enough evidence to lead them right to your door," said Jury.

Which it did.

And it was less than two weeks after the memorial service that Alice Treadnor was arrested for the murder of her husband.

It was Twickenham police, in the person of DI Dunstable, that made the arrest.

The prosecuting attorney dumped evidence on the table like the roof caving in—Tom's many threats that he was going to leave her.

Within a couple of hours, the bail bondsman arranged by Alan appeared at the jail. Alice was released on half a million pounds bond. She was to stay within a five-mile radius of Treadnor House until the trial.

# 43

Pete Apted, Q.C., looked up from the pages he'd been reading through and said to Jury, "Not with a bun on my head." Then, winding up like a pitcher, he chucked his apple core into the wastebasket.

Pete Apted was liked by very few people and admired by even fewer. Charlie Moss was the exception. She was the solicitor he turned to for any of his cases that needed one. He seemed to regard her as being indispensable and as having judgment that was unquestionable.

Carole-anne had told Jury that being questioned by Pete Apted was like being questioned by a cobra. Charlie, on the other hand, could melt into the background so that a witness thought her harmless. No one was less. Charlie could spot a lie before it was out of the suspect's mouth.

"Oh, come on, Pete," said Jury, who was sitting across the desk from him at seven o'clock the next morning. Seven o'clock was always Jury's designated time for talking to Pete Apted. "I've never known you to make a statement like that upon reading a few sentences in a document. You've not even talked to her."

"True," said Apted, "but do I want to?"

"You've got to," said Jury. "You're better than anybody else."

"That's right," said Apted. "But still, it isn't a reason for me to want to talk to Alice Treadnor. And you're saying she didn't do it."

"Of course she didn't do it," said Jury.

"Oh, really? Then why are you coming to me?"

"Because it looks so much like she did do it," said Jury.

Apted sighed heavily. "You know something, Superintendent, I think maybe you'd be better off if you just stopped talking to women altogether, because every one so far that I have known about has dealt you a losing hand."

"So you'll talk to her?" said Jury.

"Of course I'll talk to her."

Jury smiled. "I thought you would. The whole thing is so weird."

Pete Apted just looked at him and said, "You thought wrong, Superintendent. The reason I'm talking to her is not because of the weirdness, but because you asked me to. So let's say tomorrow, and I'll give you a break: You can bring her in at eight a.m. and I'll talk to her."

"Thanks," said Jury.

# 44

At eight o'clock the next morning, Jury escorted Alice Treadnor into Pete Apted's office, where Jury was surprised to see Charlie Moss sitting at one end of Apted's desk. In front of her was a glass ashtray, thus far filled with a small pile of ashes and the stub of a cigarette she had probably smoked in advance of Alice's coming in. After Jury performed the introductions, Pete Apted looked at him and said, "You're excused," as if Jury were some misbehaving student. Apted added, "Charlie can drive Mrs. Treadnor home when this is over. Thanks." Jury nodded and walked out, feeling incredibly dismissed. He was even more subverbally dismissed by Chief Superintendent Racer after Racer learned that the Twickenham business was still unsolved and suggested Jury go back to his office, again like some misbehaving schoolboy, and finish the work.

In a few hours, he got a call from Apted telling him Charlie and Alice had left and the deposition interview had been just about as much of a success as Apted had expected it to be.

Jury said, "Well frankly, I didn't know what to expect. What happened?"

"Pretty much what you thought would happen."

"Why was Charlie Moss there? She is your favorite instructing solicitor."

"That's right," said Apted. "And she'll take the case."

"What?" said Jury. "You're letting Charlie Moss handle this case?"

"Well, really, it's not a case of letting Charlie do something. Charlie believed pretty much what Alice said."

"And you didn't."

"Oh, I wouldn't trust her one inch. Not with cobweb attitudes. Emily Dickinson."

"What are you talking about, Pete?"

"She'd make a terrible witness. Not Emily, Alice. Haven't you ever found her unconvincing?"

"No, I've never tried to be convinced." That, he knew, was a total lie.

"She'd make a terrible witness. I didn't believe a word she said except hello. She was not glad at all to have met me. Treadnor Senior made it perfectly clear in his will, the twenty-million-pound trust fund would not be inherited until after Tom died. He did not trust his son. For some reason, he did trust Alice."

Jury said, "Why would Tom's father trust Alice to use that money for Land Savers?"

Apted shrugged. "Because he was a fool. I wouldn't even trust the woman to buy me a tree, much less twenty acres of forest."

Jury just stared at his office wall.

# 45

"You should have been there, Pete. Charlie Moss did an astonishing job."

"I'm sure she did," said Pete. "She always does."

"Her defense," said Jury, "was simply to take the prosecution's case, which she described as not a case but a rational explanation, and turn it on its head. She brought up in front of the jury every detail that the prosecution had mentioned. The ride on the horse from Treadnor's house to the Queen; climbing the painter's ladder to the window, through which she could get the best view of the bar; the shot at the figure on the bar stool ordinarily occupied by Tom Treadnor; then climbing back down the ladder with the rifle to the sign of the Queen, which was tilted against the side of the pub; dipping the brush in the can of red paint that the painters had left beside the sign; printing in the word "Red"; then leaving, riding the horse back to the Treadnor estate, and stashing the rifle where it was usually kept. No need to clean off the prints, since it was her rifle, and her prints would have been there anyway. Then, going into the house and going to bed. Charlie presented this as total absurdity. The whole thing. There was no case to answer, and she asked for dismissal, and she got it. It was the same thing you did with your case."

Apted interrupted. "Well, not the same, because my defendant, Jennifer Kennington, was innocent. Charlie's defendant, Alice Treadnor, is guilty as sin. That is the main difference between our two cases."

Jury looked perplexed as he stood up to leave.

"There's one more thing," said Apted as Jury was leaving the room.

Jury turned and said, "One more thing?"

"Yes," said Apted. "I was not going to tell you this, but I think I will. I have a theory about Charlie's defense."

"Theory? What is it?"

"I do not really think that was Charlie's defense. She got it from somebody else."

"Who?" said Jury. "You? You are the most likely person to think of a defense like that."

"Maybe," said Pete Apted. "But no, it was not me. It was Alice Treadnor."

Jury stopped cold. "What the hell do you mean, Pete?"

"That it was Alice Treadnor who suggested that defense. Alice Treadnor knew what a spot she was in, and that she was really the only candidate for this crime. So she worked out way ahead of time what defense could be used, and what she produced was exactly what you heard. She managed to suggest the various ridiculous scheming points that Charlie brought up, because she herself thought that such a plan would be simply unbelievable to the jury, and the jury would come back with the verdict that they came back with."

"Pete, what are you talking about?"

"It seems perfectly clear to me that Alice Treadnor knew she was going to be the prime suspect, and so she thought up this well-constructed scheme she could use and then, by way of suggestion and implication, get Charlie to use as the actual line of defense, and that's what happened. At least, I think that's what happened. I don't think Charlie came up with this. I did not think it was collusion. It was not that they thought this up together. This was originally Alice's line of defense, simply because it sounded so unlikely that no one could possibly have committed this crime this way. I mean, just look at it. Riding a horse to the scene, taking a rifle up to a window, shooting at the back of one of the customers, and—the most unbelievable of all—getting down the ladder and taking the time—taking the time, Superintendent—to write in the word 'Red' in front of 'Queen,' taking the time when the whole damn place would have been in an uproar, the police looking everywhere, inside and outside, and her with a paintbrush writing a word on a sign, and then leaving that sign, rushing to the rear of the building into the woods, where she had hitched her horse, getting on the horse, and trotting back to Treadnor House. Now really, who could believe something like that? The jury certainly did not, and Charlie knew they would not, and Alice knew that Charlie knew they wouldn't. I am sure that this was Alice's plan."

Jury stood there and stared for a moment, then spoke. "You're not kidding, are you, Pete?"

"No, Superintendent. I am not kidding, and if you are going to see Alice, as I imagine you are, why don't you ask her? Goodnight."

# 46

When Jury and Wiggins knocked at the front door of the Treadnor house, it was not Alan who opened it but Tom Treadnor himself.

Jury couldn't help himself: He stared.

"Back from the dead," Treadnor said with a smile. "Sorry to disappoint you."

Wiggins, who seemed to think his boss had gone into some sort of fugue state, said, after a brief laugh, "You certainly have a sense of humor about it, Mr. Treadnor. Sergeant Wiggins, New Scotland Yard CID." Wiggins held out his hand, which Treadnor shook. Wiggins gave Jury's foot a small kick.

Jury started and came out of his trance, also extending his hand. "Sorry, sir."

"Please come in," said Treadnor, stepping away from the door.

Alice Treadnor was waiting inside with coffee, as if this were just one more social interruption in her otherwise busy day. "So you see, Superintendent, I really didn't shoot him. In case you were still hoping."

Was the man really going to feign ignorance? Apparently.

"What possible reason could anyone have for shooting me? Unless, of course, he thought it was not me but my look-alike, Jason—what was his last name?"

"Lederer." Jury's eyes slid from the husband to the wife, who looked back at him without expression.

Tom put his arm around her shoulders. "But my God, what an ordeal for Alice!"

Alice was trying hard to look ordeal-laden but making a poor job of it. Of course, Jury had to allow for his own prejudice in this regard.

Tom squeezed her shoulder, but Alice merely stiffened, which made her, Jury thought, either a lousy actress or a lousy wife.

"Pardon me," said Wiggins, "but I'm having a hard time understanding this: First, you were murdered—or rather, Jason Lederer was. Second, your wife was tried for the shooting but the case was dismissed thanks to her brilliant defense attorney. Third, you knew nothing about all of this because of the lack of television and print media where you were." Wiggins allowed himself an exemplary laugh. "Which must have been on the moon, but even Armstrong could be reached on the moon."

"No, Sergeant, you misunderstood. I didn't say there was no TV or newspapers, only that I didn't choose to look at them."

"So, it all passed without your knowing any of it: your own murder, your wife's near-conviction—no one could get in touch with you. No one. In spite of what must have been desperate attempts to do so," said Jury.

"I'm afraid so. As I told you, it was a private island, with only helicopter service as a way on and off—"

"But, Mr. Treadnor, it was *somebody's* island."

"The somebody's name is Musa Abioye. As he's neither fluent in English nor fond of this country, he doesn't have a subscription to local or international news. He doesn't care much for me, either. I got the place through a friend of a friend."

"So I count at least three people."

"Three? For what?"

"Who knew where you were. No, make that four. We're forgetting your wife."

Treadnor, flush-faced, sat forward. "My God, Superintendent, don't you think, if I had known about all of this, I would have been back posthaste?"

"Yes. But that's begging the question, isn't it?"

There was silence.

"For example, police," said Wiggins. "Would—" he began, then, realizing he was opening a door that Treadnor could walk right through, stopped.

"You're forgetting, Sergeant. I was dead."

* * *

As Alan, who had not been there to let them in, but was certainly there to let them out, opened the door, Jury heard the Treadnors doing what they were best at: Piano keys were tinkling out a tune while ice cubes were clattering in a shaker.

What a wonderful exit act, thought Jury. "For God's sakes," he said as they were getting into the car.

"You think he's lying?"

"We *know* he's lying. And so is she. As you said, they could get a call through to Apollo 11. So the two of them cooked this up, and my guess is they worked it over for a long period of time.

As they started down the drive, Jury heard the music from the house. The piano playing was beautiful, although Jury bet that Georgia was the last thing on the minds of Tom and Alice Treadnor. He sunk down into the passenger seat, feeling suddenly sad—feeling, really, close to weeping without knowing why.

Wiggins, braking at the end of the drive, looked over at him. "Something wrong, sir?"

Jury shook his head and wiped his sleeve under his nose. "Nothing. Just an old, sweet song."

"I beg your pardon?"

"Drive."

# 47

It was Alan who opened the door for Jury and indicated that he should go into the library. Jury thanked him and said he knew the way. The library seemed to be empty; he could have sworn that no one else was there. When he looked at the gathered shadows near the French doors, he almost expected Alice to step out of them, but she wasn't there. Then he looked at the other side of the room and saw she was at the drinks table, stirring what he presumed was a pitcher of her baroque Manhattans.

As Jury walked out of the library and into the little study, he heard a soft piano version of "Waltzing Matilda" coming from the dining room. The first thing he saw in the study was a chessboard. It was not ornamental. It had weight. The meaning, of course, was to be determined. He felt he had determined nothing at all in this case. His hand moved across the chessboard. He looked at the pieces, all of them in their places. He picked up a pawn and set it on the table, then he took another, and then another.

"What are you doing?" He looked up and saw Alice standing there, looking quizzical.

He said, "Removing us."

"And who is us?"

"Well, certainly one of us is me."

"You think you're a pawn?"

"Of course." Jury laughed and returned the pawns to their places.

"I don't expect you'll join me in one of my Manhattans."

"I expect you are right. I see that you have the coffee here already."

"Yes. Sit down." He did. She walked over with her glass, which she set on the coffee table, picked up the silver pot, and poured some coffee into a very fragile-looking cup. She handed him the cup and saucer, then she sat down on the opposite side of the sofa with her drink, which she raised in a sort of toast that Jury did not answer with his coffee cup. She said, "I thought Charlie Moss was quite brilliant. Didn't you?"

"It did seem to be an extremely unique defense."

Alice said, "I couldn't in a million years have come up with anything like that."

Jury's smile was a little frosty as he answered. "You mean taking the prosecution's case and turning it around and making it the defense? No, I don't think many people would think of that, but Pete Apted has a very interesting theory about the whole procedure. Pete thinks the idea was not Charlie Moss's."

"Then whose was it? Was it Pete Apted's?"

"Oh, no. No. It was yours."

"Mine?" With her intake of breath, the glass in her hand tilted and a little of the drink spilled on the table. She snatched up the napkin on the tray and mopped it up.

"I don't know what you're talking about."

"Then I'll explain."

"Oh, please do."

"Apted says the story that Charlie Moss told the jury was actually true. It's what happened. You left your house on horseback. You rode to the rear of the Queen, tied up the horse, went around to the ladder, and climbed the few rungs to the window that would allow you the best view of the customers at the bar, one of whom was Jason Lederer."

Alice interrupted. "Wait. The arrangement was it should be Tom sitting on that bar stool. Not Jason Lederer—"

"The plan had changed. You made a new arrangement, and Lederer was not aware of it. Treadnor Senior made it perfectly clear in his will that the twenty-million-pound trust fund would not be inherited until after Tom died. He did not trust his son. For some reason, he did trust you. The arrangement, said Jury, was to pay an enormous sum to this Lederer guy, and to have him sit at Tom's place at the bar. You needed a rotter, someone like Lederer to take the bait and fall for your scheme to execute your plan.

"So you shot him. You descended the ladder and, remarkably, you decided to write in the word 'Red' before 'Queen.' Even though chaos had pretty much taken over, you did this anyway, as it was part of your unbelievable story. Then, you collected your rifle. You made your way back to the woods and the horse, and you galloped or cantered back to the stables at Treadnor's house. And that was it."

This time she spilled her Manhattan when she stood up and said, "Richard, what are you talking about?"

He said, "Oh, please. Don't keep it up, Alice. Pete knows you're guilty."

"But you seem to be implying—"

"I'm not implying, Alice. He knew you were guilty because you are. Because this was a deliberate attempt to construct exactly the kind of story that would result in the court dismissing the case. It was simply too outlandish to work as a defense. Nobody would believe it. And you knew when you made it up that nobody would believe it. You know something, Alice? I think it's really quite amusing that your name is Alice. Little Alice falling down the rabbit hole and not knowing what is there and having nothing about her but confusion. When indeed, your name should have been 'The Red Queen': that calculating, cold